"Um, what are you doing?" she asked as she realized what was happening.

"I'm getting this out of the way." Sebastian shrugged off his dress shirt and stepped out of the suit pants that had pooled at his feet. "We can't spend this whole week tiptoeing around each other. We're sharing a room. Sharing a bed. It doesn't matter what does or doesn't happen in the bed—we need to be more comfortable around each other." Standing in nothing but those same navy boxer briefs, Sebastian held out his arms.

"Take a good look. Get it out of your system. It's just the standard equipment."

Harper watched with confusion and curiosity as he displayed himself to her. His equipment was anything but standard.

Sebastian sought out a pair of lounging pants from his bag. He tugged them on and looked at her with a wry grin. "Now when you talk to your girlfriends about getting me out of my pants, you don't have to lie."

* * *

The Boyfriend Arrangement
is part of the Millionaires of Manhattan series
from Andrea Laurence!

Dear Reader,

When I was plotting the stories for these Yale sorority sisters almost two years ago, I already knew Harper's secret. The readers wouldn't know the truth, just like her friends and family, but it was there, coloring her every interaction with the world. As a writer, I love knowing things about my characters, even details that never make it to the page. It makes them more real to me. I couldn't wait for Harper's book, where she would finally be able to free herself with the truth.

I also knew her hero had a secret of his own, but I didn't know what it would be until I found myself in the cardiac care unit of my local hospital with someone very important to me. As a writer, every experience—good or bad—is a potential research opportunity. When I learned more about coronary artery disease than I ever wanted to know, I funneled it into the current book I was writing and just like that, Sebastian developed a secret heart problem.

Thankfully, things turned out well for my own cardiac patient and I was glad to write a happy ending for Harper and Sebastian, too. If you enjoy Harper and Sebastian's story, tell me by visiting my website at andrealaurence.com, like my fan page on Facebook or follow me on Twitter. I'd love to hear from you!

Enjoy,

Andrea

ANDREA LAURENCE

THE BOYFRIEND ARRANGEMENT

 HARLEQUIN® DESIRE

Recycling programs
for this product may
not exist in your area.

ISBN-13: 978-1-335-97182-1

The Boyfriend Arrangement

Copyright © 2018 by Andrea Laurence

Printed in U.S.A.

Andrea Laurence is an award-winning author of contemporary romances filled with seduction and sass. She has been a lover of reading and writing stories since she was young. A dedicated West Coast girl transplanted into the deep south, she is thrilled to share her special blend of sensuality and dry, sarcastic humor with readers.

Books by Andrea Laurence

Harlequin Desire

Brides and Belles

Snowed In with Her Ex
Thirty Days to Win His Wife
One Week with the Best Man
A White Wedding Christmas

Millionaires of Manhattan

What Lies Beneath
More Than He Expected
His Lover's Little Secret
The CEO's Unexpected Child
Little Secrets: Secretly Pregnant
Rags to Riches Baby
One Unforgettable Weekend
The Boyfriend Arrangement

Visit her Author Profile page at Harlequin.com, or andrealaurence.com, for more titles.

One

"You have got to be kidding me!"

Sebastian West scanned his proximity card for the third time and yet the front door of BioTech—the biomedical technology company he co-founded—refused to open. Seeing his employees moving around inside, he pounded his fist on the glass, but all of them ignored him.

"I own this company!" he shouted as his secretary walked by without making eye contact. "Don't make me fire you, Virginia."

At that, she came to a stop and circled back to the door.

"Finally," he sighed.

But she didn't open the door as he'd expected. Instead she just shook her head. "I'm under strict orders from Dr. Solomon not to open the door for you, sir."

"Oh, come on," he groaned.

She couldn't be moved. "You'll have to take it up with him, sir." Then she turned on her heel and disappeared.

"Finn!" he shouted at the top of his lungs, pounding on the glass with angry fists. "Let me in, you son of a bitch."

A moment later Sebastian's former college roommate and business partner, Finn Solomon, appeared at the door with a frown on his face. "You're supposed to be on vacation," he said through the glass.

"That's what the doctor said, yeah, but since when do I take vacations? Or listen to doctors?" The answer was never. He certainly never listened to Finn. And as for vacation, he hadn't taken one in the decade since they'd started this company. You couldn't be off lying on a beach and also breaking barriers in medical technology. The two were incompatible.

"That's the whole point, Sebastian. Do you not recall that you had a heart attack two days ago? You're not supposed to be in the office for a minimum of two weeks."

"A mild heart attack. They didn't keep me in the hospital for more than a few hours. And they're not even sure I really had one. I'm taking the stupid pills they gave me, what more do you want?"

"I want you to go home. I'm not letting you in.

I've had your badge deactivated. I've also sent out a memo that anyone who lets you in the building will be terminated."

So much for piggybacking through the door behind someone else. He did have a laptop, though, if he could get Virginia to bring it out to him. That wouldn't technically be breaking the rules if he worked from home, right?

"I've also had your email and remote access accounts temporarily suspended, so you can't even work from home." Finn was always remarkably good at reading his mind. He'd been able to do it since they were in college. It was great for working together. Not so great for this scenario. "You are on mandatory medical leave, Sebastian, and as a doctor, I'm sorry, but I'm going to enforce it. I can handle things for two weeks, but I can't run this company with you dead. So get some R and R. Take a trip. Get a massage. Get a hand job. I really don't care. But I don't want to see you here."

Sebastian was at a loss. He and Finn had started this company after school, pouring their hearts and souls into technology that could make people's lives better. He was the MIT engineer and Finn was the doctor, a winning team that had developed advanced technologies like prosthetic hands and electric wheelchairs controlled by a patient's brain waves. That seemed a noble enough cause to dedicate his life to.

But apparently a decade of trading sleep and vegetables for caffeine and sugar had caught up with him.

Of course he didn't want to die; he was only thirty-eight. But he was close to a breakthrough on a robotic exoskeleton that could make paraplegics like his brother walk again.

"What about the new prototype for the exo-legs?"

Finn just crossed his huge forearms over his chest. "Those people have gone a long time without walking. They can wait two more weeks while you recover. If you keel over at your desk one afternoon, they'll never get it. As it is, I'm having a defibrillator installed on the wall outside your office."

Sebastian sighed, knowing he'd lost this fight. Finn was just as stubborn as he was. Normally that was a good match—they never knew when to take no for an answer. But that wouldn't benefit him in this situation. He knew the doctor's orders, yet he'd never once imagined that Finn would enforce them this strictly. He'd just thought he'd work ten-hour days instead of the usual eighteen.

"Can I at least come in and—?"

"*No*," Finn interrupted. "Go home. Go shopping. Just go away." With a smug expression Finn waved at him through the glass and then turned his back on his business partner.

Sebastian stood there for a moment, thinking maybe Finn would come back and tell him he was just kidding. When it was clear that Finn was deadly serious, he wandered back to the elevator and returned to the lobby of the building. He stepped out onto the busy Manhattan sidewalk with no real clue as to where he was going to go. He'd planned to take it easy for a few days and head back to work today. Now he had two full weeks of nothingness ahead of him.

He had the resources to do almost anything on earth that he wanted. Fly to Paris on a private jet. Take a luxury cruise through the Caribbean. Sing karaoke in Tokyo. He just didn't want to do any of those things.

Money was an alien thing to Sebastian. Unlike Finn, he'd never had it growing up. His parents had worked hard but as blue collar laborers they'd just never seemed to get ahead. And after his brother Kenny's ATV accident, they'd gone from poor to near destitute under the weight of the medical bills.

Scholarships and loans had gotten Sebastian through college, after which he'd focused on building his company with Finn. The company eventually brought money—lots of it—but he'd been really too busy to notice. Or to spend any. He'd never dreamed of traveling or owning expensive sports cars. Honestly, he was bad at being rich. He probably didn't even have twenty bucks in his wallet.

Stopping at a street corner, he pulled his wallet out of his back pocket and noticed the leather had nearly disintegrated over the years. He'd probably had this one since grad school. Maybe he should consider getting a new one. He had nothing better to do at the moment.

Up ahead, he spied Neiman Marcus. Surely they sold wallets. He made his way across the street and over to the department store. Sebastian stopped long enough to hold the door for a group of attractive women exiting with enough bags to put a kid through a semester or two of college. They looked vaguely familiar, especially the last one with the dark hair and steely blue eyes.

Her gaze flicked over him for a moment and he felt it like a punch to his gut. His pulse pounded in his throat as he tried to unsuccessfully swallow the lump that had formed there. He didn't know why he would have such a visceral reaction to the woman. He wanted to say something but he couldn't place the woman and decided to keep his mouth shut. Half a second later she looked away, breaking the connection, and continued on down the street with her friends.

Sebastian watched them for a moment with a touch of regret, then forced himself into the store. He made a beeline for the men's department and quickly selected a wallet. He wasn't particularly choosy with that sort of thing. He just wanted black leather and a slim profile with enough room for a couple cards and some cash. Easy.

As he found a register open for checkout, he noticed a strikingly attractive brunette ahead of him. Sebastian realized she was one of the women he'd just seen leave the store a few minutes before. The one with the blue-gray eyes. He wished he remembered who she was so he could say something to her. They'd probably met at one event or another around town—Finn forced him to go to the occasional party or charity gala—he couldn't be sure, though. Most of his brain was allocated to robotics and engineering.

Not all of it, though. He was red-blooded male enough to notice her tall, lean figure, long, chestnut hair, big blue eyes and bloodred lips. It was impossible not to notice how flawlessly she was put together. She smelled like the meadow behind his childhood home after a warm summer rain. Deep down inside him something clenched tightly at the thought.

What was it about her? He told himself it was probably nothing to do with her, exactly. The doctor had told him to refrain from strenuous physical activity—*Yes, that includes sexual relations, Mr. West*—for at least a week. It had been a while since he'd indulged with a lady, but maybe since it was forbidden, his mind was focusing on what it couldn't have.

Why was he so terrible at remembering names?

As Sebastian got closer to the counter, he realized the woman was returning everything in her bag. That was odd. If the register was correct, she'd just purchased and immediately returned about fifteen hundred dollars' worth of clothes. He watched as she slipped out of her leather coat and shoved it into the empty department store bag, covering it with the packing tissue so you couldn't see inside.

His chronic boredom was temporarily interrupted as she piqued his curiosity with her actions. "Excuse m—" he started to say.

She turned suddenly and slammed right into his chest, forcing him to reach out and catch her in his arms before she stumbled backward on her sky-high heels and fell to the ground. He pulled her tight against him, molding her breasts to his chest until she righted herself. He found he really didn't want to let go when the time came. He was suddenly drunk on her scent and the feel of her soft curves pressing into his hard angles. How long had it been since he'd been this close to a woman? One he wasn't fitting a prosthetic to? He had no clue.

But eventually he did let go.

The woman took an unsteady step back, pulling herself together with a crimson flush blooming across her cheeks. "I am so sorry about that," she said. "I'm always in such a hurry that I don't pay attention to where I'm going."

There was a faint light of recognition in her blue-gray eyes as she looked up at him, so he knew he was right about meeting her somewhere before. "No, don't apologize," he said with a wry smile. "That's the most exciting thing to happen to me all week."

Her brow furrowed in disbelief.

Perhaps, he mused, he didn't look as boring as he was.

"Are you okay?" she asked.

He laughed off her concern. She was tall for a woman, especially in those stilettos, but he didn't really think she could inflict damage to him. "I'm fine. I'm just glad I was able to catch you."

She smirked and looked down self-consciously. "I suppose it could've been worse."

"You actually look really familiar to me, but I'm horrible with names. I'm Sebastian West," he said, offering her his hand in greeting.

She accepted it tentatively. The touch of her smooth skin gliding along his sent an unexpected spark through his nervous system. He was usually focused on work, and other pursuits, like sexual gratification and dating in general, typically took the back burner. But with one simple touch, physical desire was moved to the forefront.

Unlike their brief collision, this touch lingered skin-to-skin, letting him enjoy the flickers of electricity across his palm. The connection between them was palpable. So much so that when she pulled her hand away, she rubbed it gently on her burgundy sweater as if to dull the sensation.

"You do look familiar," she agreed. "I'm Harper Drake. We must've met around town. Perhaps you know my brother Oliver? Orion Computers?"

That sounded familiar enough. "He's probably

pals with my friend Finn Solomon. Finn knows everyone."

Harper narrowed her eyes for a moment, looking thoughtful. "That name sounds familiar, too. Wait… are you involved in some kind of medical supply business?"

Sebastian's brows rose in surprise. That wasn't exactly how he'd categorize what he did, but the fact that she remembered that much stunned him. And, to be honest, it pleased him just a little bit.

"You could say that." He grinned.

Harper beamed. She was pleased to finally place this guy in her mind. When she'd caught a glimpse of him earlier, he'd grabbed her attention. He'd looked so familiar when he'd held the door for her that she was certain she'd known him from somewhere. Unfortunately, Violet being so hell-bent on running up the street to pick up Aidan's wedding present had meant she couldn't stop.

Once she'd split from her best friends, Lucy Drake, Violet Niarchos and Emma Flynn, she'd stealthily circled back to Neiman Marcus to return everything she'd just bought. She couldn't have that weighing down her credit card for long. She hadn't expected to run into the familiar man again. Certainly not literally.

Real smooth, Harper.

"Okay, well then, I think it must've been one of the hospital benefits this past winter."

He nodded. "I do think I went to one of those. Finn tries to get me out every now and then."

Sebastian West didn't have a face she could forget, even if she lost context. He had a strong jaw, a nearly jet-black goatee, eyes just as dark, and a crooked smile that stirred something inside her. No, she'd remember him for sure. If she had a type, he'd be it.

It was a shame he wasn't one of the rich CEO guys her brother associated with all the time. She didn't mean to be shallow, but meeting a guy with his act together financially would certainly benefit her current situation. It would also make her feel a little better about how things would be handled once it all changed on her birthday.

The last seven years had been one long, hard lesson learned for Harper. One in the value of money the spoiled little rich girl she'd once been had never really experienced before. She would be the first to admit that her father had basically given her everything she'd wanted. After her mother died, he'd spoiled her. And continued to spoil her until he'd no longer had the resources.

Harper had never imagined that the well would run dry. When it had, she'd made a lot of necessary adjustments in her life. At least secretly. It was embarrassing enough that she'd blown all the money she'd inherited when she'd turned eighteen—especially since she was an accountant—she didn't need anyone else knowing about what she'd done.

After falling from the top of the world to her current spot near the bottom, she'd earned a whole new appreciation for money and for the people who were good at managing it. And soon, when she had money again, she intended to be very careful about how she handled it. That included triple-checking every guy she dated. Not that she intended to date Sebastian…

"Well, I'm glad we bumped into each other today," Sebastian said with a sly grin.

Harper chuckled. As her gaze broke away from Sebastian's for a moment, she saw Quentin—her ex, of all people—walking toward them. Grabbing Sebastian's arm, she turned them both toward a display of men's shoes, hoping maybe Quentin hadn't seen her. "I'm sorry," she muttered under her breath. "I'm trying to—"

"Harper?"

Damn it.

Harper turned to face the ex-boyfriend she'd done her best to avoid for the last two years. She stepped away from Sebastian, leaning in to give her ex a polite but stiff hug. "Hello, Quentin," she said in a flat, disinterested tone she knew he wouldn't pick up on. He never did.

"How have you been?"

Lonely. Anxiety-riddled. "I'm great. Never better. How about you?"

"Amazing. I actually just got engaged."

Engaged? Quentin was engaged. The one who didn't want to commit. If Harper hadn't already been feeling crappy about being the last single friend in her social circle, this moment would've been the straw that broke the camel's back. She pasted a fake smile on her face and nodded. "That's great. I'm happy for you."

Quentin didn't notice her lack of sincerity. "Thank you. Her name is Josie. She's amazing. I can't wait for you to meet her. I think you two would really get along."

Harper had to bite her tongue to keep from asking why his ex would have any interest in hanging out with his fiancée. "I'm sure we would."

"So, Harper…" Quentin said as he leaned in to her. His arrogant smile made her shoulders tense and the scent of his stinky, expensive cologne brought to mind nights with him she wished she could forget. "Will I be seeing you at Violet's wedding? It's the event of the year, I hear. I can't believe she's flying all the guests to Dublin for it. And renting out a castle! It's wild. Maybe I should've dated her instead of you." He chuckled and she curled her hands into fists at her sides.

"I am going," she said with a bright smile she hoped didn't betray her anxiety over the upcoming trip. "I'm one of her bridesmaids."

"Are you going alone?" Quentin cocked his head

in a sympathetically curious way that made her hackles rise.

Why would he assume she was going alone? They'd been apart for two years. He'd moved on. Surely she could've found someone to replace him by now. She hadn't, but she could've. "No. I'm not going alone. I'm bringing my boyfriend."

The minute the words passed her lips she regretted them. Why had she said that? Why? He mentions a fiancée and she loses her damn mind. She didn't have a boyfriend. She hadn't even committed to a houseplant. How was she supposed to produce a boyfriend in a couple days before the trip?

Quentin's eyes narrowed in disbelief. "Oh, really? I hadn't heard you were dating anyone lately."

Harper was surprised that he'd been paying attention. "I've learned to keep my private life private," she snapped. After their messy, public breakup, it had been another lesson hard learned. She hadn't even considered dating for six months after they'd ended due to the trauma of the whole thing.

"Well, who's the lucky guy? Do I know him? I look forward to meeting him at the wedding."

A name. She needed a name. Harper's mind went completely blank. Looking around the department store, her gaze fell on Sebastian as he perused a nearby display of dress loafers.

"You can meet him now. Sebastian, honey, could

you come over here for a minute? I'd like you to meet someone."

Sebastian arched his brow inquisitively at Harper as she mouthed the word "please" silently to him. He wandered over to where she was standing. "Yes, *dear*?"

"Sebastian, this is my ex, Quentin Stuart. I've mentioned him, haven't I? Anyway, I was just telling him about the two of us going to Ireland for Violet and Aidan's wedding."

Quentin stuck out his hand to Sebastian. "Nice to meet you, Sebastian…?"

"West. Sebastian West." He shook Quentin's hand and quickly pulled his away.

"Sebastian West as in BioTech?"

"Actually, yes."

Harper didn't recognize the name of the company, but then again she didn't know much about Sebastian because they weren't really dating. She remembered a brief discussion at a party about him working in medical supplies and how he didn't get out very much. She'd figured he'd sold wheelchairs and hospital beds or something. Maybe she'd been wrong. Quentin wasn't the type to waste brain power on remembering things that didn't impress him.

"Wow, Harper. Quite the catch you've got in this one." An uncomfortable expression flickered across his face and quickly disappeared. "Well, I've got to run. I was on my way to meet Josie and I'm already late. I'll see you two lovebirds on the plane to Dublin. I look forward to speaking with you some more, Sebastian."

Harper watched Quentin walk out of the store. Once he was gone, her face dropped into her hands. She just knew she was bright red with embarrassment. "I am so sorry," she muttered through her fingers.

Sebastian surprised her by laughing. "Want to tell me what that was all about?"

She peeked through her hands at him. "Um… Quentin is my ex. It was a messy breakup, but we still hang in the same social circles from time to time. When he asked about my date for the wedding we have coming up, I panicked. I told him you were my boyfriend. It's a long story. I shouldn't have dragged you into that, but he put me on the spot and you were standing right there." She gestured toward the display and shook her head. "I'm an ass."

"I doubt that," Sebastian said, a twinkle of laughter still in his dark brown eyes.

"No, I am. I've made the whole thing ten times worse because now I'm going to show up at the wedding without you and he's going to know I lied. And I just know he's going to show up with his beautiful, new fiancée and I'm going to feel even more like crap than I already do."

Harper knew she should've just owned that she was single. How bad would that have been? To just state proudly that she'd been dating and not interested in settling down or settling on the wrong guy. She was almost thirty, but that was hardly the end of the world. In fact, *her* thirtieth birthday couldn't come soon enough. It brought a twenty-eight-million-dollar payout with it that she was desperate to get her hands on.

"Don't worry about what he thinks," Sebastian said. "He seems like a schmuck."

"I'm no good at the boyfriend thing. I have questionable taste in men," Harper admitted. "It's probably better that I just make up boyfriends instead of finding another real one."

Sebastian nodded awkwardly. "I'm glad to help. Well, I hope the wedding goes well for you."

"Thanks." She watched him leave. But with every step he took, the more panicked she became. She had no easy way of contacting this guy once he walked out the door. She didn't want to let him get away quite yet for reasons she wasn't ready to think about. "Sebastian?" she nearly shouted before he got out of earshot.

He stopped and turned back to her. "Yes?"

"How would you like to go on an all-expenses-paid trip to Ireland?"

Two

Sebastian didn't know what to say. He'd never had a woman offer him a vacation, much less a woman he hardly knew. Actually he didn't have women offer him much of anything. It was impossible when he never left the lab. The only woman he was ever around on a daily basis was his assistant, Virginia, who was in her late fifties and married.

"Um, run that by me again?"

Harper closed the gap between them with an apologetic smile on her face and a sultry sway of her hips. So many of her features were almost masculine in a way, with piercing eyes, sharp cheekbones and an aquiline nose, but there was nothing masculine about her. Her dark brows were arched delicately over eyes that were like the stormy seas off Maine where he was born.

He imagined a similar maelstrom was stirring inside her to make an offer like that to a complete stranger. Surely she could find a romantic interest if she wanted one. But he was willing to say yes to almost anything she offered when she looked at him that way.

"My friends are getting married in Ireland next weekend. They're flying everyone there, plus putting all the guests up in a castle that's been converted into a hotel. It wouldn't cost you anything to go but some leave from work. I'm not sure what your boss is like, since this is short notice, but I was hoping you would be interested."

"In going to Ireland?"

She nodded. "With me. As my boyfriend. I just introduced you to Quentin as my boyfriend and said you were going, so he's going to expect you to be there."

His brow furrowed. Her boyfriend. For a week. In Ireland. What could go wrong? Absolutely everything. Pretending to be her lover could be complicated. But what could go right? His gaze raked over her tall, lean figure with appreciation. Everything could go very right, too.

Wait—*crap*—he wasn't supposed to be "active." Just his damn luck. "Just to be clear—are you wanting or expecting you and me to…um…"

"No!" Harper was quick to answer with wide eyes. "I mean, not for real. We'd have to pretend to be a couple around everyone else—kiss, be affectionate, you know. But when we're alone, I promise it's strictly hands off. I'm not that hard up. I just can't go to this thing alone. Not after seeing Quentin and finding out he's engaged. I just can't."

Sebastian blinked his eyes a few times and tried to mask some of his disappointment. He wasn't sure if he could stand being around her, touching her in public and then just flipping the switch when they were alone. The doctor wanted him to, but he wasn't the best at following doctor's orders.

This day had done well to throw him off his game. First, getting locked out at work with mandatory vacation and now this. A beautiful woman wanted him to travel with her to Ireland for free and pretend to be her lover. That just wasn't business as usual for him. He wasn't entirely sure what to say to her. It seemed foolish to say yes and downright stupid to say no.

"I'll pay you two thousand dollars to go. It's all the money I have in my savings account," Harper added, sweetening the pot as she seemed to sense his hesitation.

She was serious. Her insecurity struck him as odd considering how confident and put together she seemed. He wasn't sure why this was so important to her. There must be more to the situation with her ex than she was telling. "Aren't your friends going to wonder where I came from? You've never spoken about me before and suddenly I'm your wedding date?"

Harper waved away his concern. "I'll take care of that. My friends have been so wrapped up in their own lives lately they'd probably not notice if I did have a boyfriend. They certainly haven't mentioned that I don't have one."

"And why is that?" Sebastian couldn't stop himself from asking. But if he was going to pretend to be her boyfriend, he needed to know if there was something about her that repelled men. From where he was standing, he didn't see a thing wrong with her. She was beautiful, well-spoken, poised and polished. Aside from the slight hint of desperation in her voice, she seemed like quite the catch. There had to be something wrong with her.

She shrugged and sort of fidgeted before responding, showing the first sign of vulnerability, which he was glad to see. "Like I said, I don't have the best taste in men. Things haven't worked out with anyone I've been attracted to since Quentin and I broke up."

"You can't find a decent man to go to dinner with you, but you trust me enough to travel across the ocean with you, share a bedroom and make out in front of your friends?" There was a flaw in her logic here. "I could be crazy. Or a criminal. Or married. I could attack you in your sleep or steal your jewelry. The possibilities are endless."

Harper scoffed at his trepidations. "Honestly, I take that risk on every date I go on in this town. Have you seen the guys on Tinder lately? No…you probably haven't." She chuckled. "I know you have a job, you smell nice, you're handsome and you went along with my lie just now, so you're easygoing. You're already a head and shoulders over every date I've had in the last six months. If you don't want to go, or can't, just say so. But don't turn it down because you're concerned about my blatant disregard for my own welfare or poor sense of judgment. My friends are already well aware of that flaw in my character."

"No, I can go. As of this morning my schedule is amazingly wide open for the next two weeks." That was an understatement. But was this what he should spend his time doing? He didn't exactly have a more tempting offer.

"Do you find me physically repulsive?"

Sebastian swallowed hard. "Not at all. To the contrary, you're the most beautiful woman I've laid eyes on in a very long time."

Harper's eyes widened a touch at his answer, but she quickly recovered with a sly smile curling her lips. It must have boosted her confidence because she moved a step closer to him, closing the gap until they were nearly touching. "Do you think you'd have trouble pretending to be my lover? Or have a problem kissing me?"

Every muscle in Sebastian's body tightened as

she spoke. The warmth of her body and the scent of her so close caused an instant physical reaction that would answer any of her questions if she bothered to notice. He balled his hands into fists at his sides to keep from reaching for her. He'd craved the sensation of touching her again since the moment he'd let her go after the collision.

He shook his head stiffly. "No. I think I can manage that."

Harper's gaze never left his. "Okay, great. Are you opposed to a free trip to Europe? You have a passport, right?"

"I have a passport, yes." It had no stamps in it, but he had one. Finn did most of the travel around the world, schmoozing on behalf of their company. Sebastian kept his nose in his paperwork and schematics, but Finn had made him get a passport anyway.

"Okay. Then I see no reason why you shouldn't say yes."

Neither did he. Why was he making this so hard?

It really was a simple thing. He had no reason not to go. All he had to do was walk around Ireland with this stunning woman on his arm. He had no intention of taking her money, but a trip would be a nice distraction without any work on his plate for the next few weeks. What else was he going to do? Finn was right that he could help more people healthy than dead, but taking a break was hard for him. Being a couple thousand miles from his work would make it easier.

"When do you leave for the wedding?"

"Monday afternoon."

"It's Friday morning. Three days? Are you serious? Won't your friend think it odd that you're suddenly adding a guest to her wedding on such short notice?"

"Not really. I RSVP'd for two. I just needed to find my plus one."

"You're cutting it awfully close. Desperate?"

"I prefer to think of it as optimistic."

"Three days…" he repeated. Something about this whole situation struck him as insane, but there was a fine line between insanity and genius.

"So does your silent resignation mean you're at least considering coming with me?" Harper grinned wide, her whole expression lighting up with excitement.

It was hard for him to turn her down when she looked at him like that. He wanted her to keep looking at him that way for as long as possible. "Well, yes, I am. I'm just not sure I'll make a very good boyfriend, fake or otherwise. I'm kinda out of practice."

"I'm not worried about that." Harper leaned into him and wrapped her arms around his neck in an unexpectedly intimate way. His whole body stiffened as she pressed against him. "You know what they say."

Sebastian took a deep breath and tried to wish

away the sudden rush of desire that coursed through his veins as she stood close. It seemed wrong to react like this to a woman he'd just met, despite how easily she was able to coax it out of him. "What's th-that?" He stuttered in his response, something he hadn't done since elementary school. She had managed to get under his skin so quickly.

"Practice makes perfect."

He nodded. "I've heard that."

Harper frowned, lowered her arms and looked down to where his hands were tensely curled at his sides. She took them in her own and moved each one to rest at the curve of her hips. "Relax, Sebastian. I'm not going to bite. We've got to be a lot more comfortable touching each other if we're going to convince anyone we're really together."

He splayed his fingers across her denim-clad hips and pressed the tips into the ample flesh there. With her so close, he wanted to lean down and kiss her. Her full, pouting lips and wide, innocent eyes seemed to plead for it. Indulging seemed like the natural thing to do. She felt good against him. Perhaps too good for the middle of Neiman Marcus. There was definitely not going to be a problem faking attraction with Harper. The problem would be pretending that the attraction wasn't real when no one was watching.

"I'll go," he blurted out, almost surprising himself.

Harper stiffened in his arms, looking up at him

with a smile that was hesitant to believe him. "Are you serious?"

Sebastian nodded. "Yes, I'm serious. I'll go to Ireland with you as your fake boyfriend."

With a squeal of excitement, Harper hugged him tight. Before he could prepare himself, she pressed her mouth to his. He was certain it was supposed to be a quick, thank-you peck, but once their lips touched, there was no pulling away.

Sebastian wasn't imagining the palpable sexual energy between them. The way Harper curved against his body and opened her mouth to him was proof of that. He wanted to take it further, to see how powerful their connection really was, but this was neither the time nor the place, so he pulled away while he still could.

Harper lingered close, a rosy flush highlighting her cheeks. "Listen, I've got to go. Would you care to walk me to my apartment? I don't live far."

"I can't." He wanted to—quite badly—but he got the feeling it was an invitation better declined at the moment if they were going to spend the next week together. Things could get weird before they even left.

Harper pulled away just enough to let a chill of air rush in where the heat of her body had been. "Why not?"

He picked up the wallet he'd set down on a display when he'd spoken with Quentin. "I still have to buy this."

A light of amusement lit her eyes. "You're so literal. I can wait while you check out."

It would be so easy to say yes. He took a deep breath and thought up another valid reason. "I also have some things to take care of if I'm going with you on Monday."

Harper pouted for a moment before she nodded and covered her disappointment with a smile. "Okay. Well, I'm going out with my girlfriends tomorrow, but how about we get together on Sunday night? We can get to know each other a little better before we get on the plane."

"At your apartment?"

"A bar is probably a better idea. Being you're a stranger and all, right?"

He breathed a sigh of relief. He could avoid temptation in a bar. Once they got to Ireland, he wasn't so sure. "That sounds good."

"Give me your phone."

Sebastian handed over his cell phone and Harper put her information into his contacts.

"Text me so I have your information, too. We'll get together Sunday."

With a smile and a wave, Harper handed over his phone and disappeared from the store. Sebastian watched her walk away and, with every step she took, was more and more convinced that he was making a big mistake.

* * *

"I know that we're leaving Monday and I should probably be packing or getting ready, but I really needed one last girls' night before we go." Violet eased back into the sofa cushions with a large glass of wine in her hand. "Why didn't any of you tell me how stressful weddings could be?"

"Well, Oliver and I eloped, so it wasn't stressful at all," Lucy said. "Besides, in the end it's just a party. Now, nine-month-old twins…that's stressful."

Harper chuckled at her new sister-in-law's observation. The twins—Alice and Christian—were little darlings, but the minute they started walking, she got the feeling they would be tiny tornadoes of destruction. Especially Alice. She was a little spitfire, like her namesake, their great-great-aunt Alice.

"No one said you had to fly all your friends and family halfway around the world to get married," Harper pointed out, taking a sip of her wine. "You could've had a ridiculously expensive and over-the-top affair here in Manhattan like Emma did."

Emma came into the room with a frown pulling down the corners of her flawlessly painted rose lips. "My wedding was not over the top. It was small and tasteful."

Harper arched an eyebrow and laughed. "You may have only had thirty people there, but I'd hardly classify it as small and tasteful."

"I had a beautiful reception."

"You had an ice vodka luge," Harper challenged.

Emma twisted her lips and sighed. "That was Jonah's thing. He insisted." She settled beside Violet on the couch. "And it would've been ten times bigger if my mother'd had her way. You saw what she did with my baby shower. But seriously, don't stress too badly about the wedding, Vi. It's in Ireland. In a castle! It will be beautiful, I promise."

"It will," Lucy chimed in. "You've got an amazing wedding planner who has it under control. The best in the city. All you need to do is show up and marry the love of your life. That's easy."

Violet smiled. "You're right. Aidan has told me the same thing a dozen times. I just can't stop stressing out about every little detail. In a week from today I'll be Mrs. Aidan Murphy! Have I forgotten something?"

"If you have, it doesn't really matter. As long as both of you show up, say I do and sign your license with a qualified officiant, you'll be married at the end of the day. Everything else is just details," Emma said.

Violet nodded. "You're right. I know you're right. I just need to say it until I believe it. What about you guys? Are you packed and ready to leave yet?"

The women around the coffee table nodded. "Everything is ready. Just a few more things to throw in the luggage before we go. We're leaving the twins with Oliver's dad," Lucy said. "That's the biggest stressor for me. I haven't been away from them since they were born, but there's no way I'm flying overseas with twins at that age.

"Knox is older than the twins, so I'm hoping he does okay on the flight. It will be his first," Violet explained. "I couldn't leave him behind, though. It seems wrong to marry his father without having him there."

"Of course. I'm sure he'll do great. Georgette is staying with my parents, but they'll have her nanny with them, so I'm not worried." Emma turned to Harper. "What about you? Are you ready to go? At least you don't have men and kids to wrangle before the trip. I almost forget what it's like to just have to worry about myself."

"Yep," Harper said. She took a deep breath and prepared herself to tell the story she'd come up with after talking to Sebastian. Her intention was to tell them as little as possible, but she knew she had to fill the girls in on her new beau before the trip. They were the only ones who would really care. If she sold the story to them, everyone else would take it at face value.

Including Quentin. Hopefully. If he didn't buy it, there was no point in continuing the ruse. This whole ridiculous scheme was designed with the sole purpose of making him believe she had someone in her life. That she wasn't pathetically single and still pining for him. Because she was anything but pining. She was glad to have Quentin out of her life. He was just too egomaniacal to see her single status as anything other than a reflection of her wishing they were still together.

Selling it to her friends wouldn't be so easy, though.

"I've got the dress, the passport and…uh…the boyfriend all ready to go." She said the words quickly and then waited for the inevitable response.

Emma, Violet and Lucy all paused as anticipated and turned to look at her. The questions came too fast and furiously for her to respond to any of them.

"What?"

"Your boyfriend?"

"Am I missing something, here?"

Harper winced and nodded when they finally quieted down. "Yeah, um, his name is Sebastian." She got up to refill her wine and stall the conversation a moment. She was going to need some alcohol to get through this conversation. When she came back into the room from the kitchen, the girls were sitting frozen in place with expectant looks on their faces. "He's the guy I've been seeing for a few months."

"Months?" Violet wailed. "You've been seeing a guy for *months* and didn't think to mention it to us?"

"You guys have all been busy with your own lives. Babies, weddings…" Harper explained. "And, to be honest, I didn't want to jinx it. It wasn't that serious at first and I got tired of mentioning guys to you all and then we didn't get past the third date. Things were going well, so I wasn't ready to talk about him yet. Just in case."

"And now you're ready to talk? 'Cause you're sure as hell going to give us every detail," Lucy sassed.

Harper shrugged. Not really, but the time had come to spill some information if she was going to pull this off. "I guess I have to if I want to bring him on the trip."

"I noticed you RSVP'd for two, but you left off the guest's name," Violet said. "I was wondering what that meant."

"Yeah, I was hopeful that things would work out for him to come," Harper continued to lie, noting that after pretending she had money for a decade, pretending to have a boyfriend wasn't as hard as she'd thought it would be. "But if it fell apart between us, I thought I might bring a friend. Or no one. But things are great and so Sebastian is coming. I'll give you his information to add to the travel manifest."

"I'm eager to meet him," Emma said. "And intrigued. You haven't really had much luck dating since you and Quentin broke up. Where did you two meet? He's not one of your Tinder finds, is he?"

"Oh, no. Those were a mess. I actually met Sebastian at one of the hospital fund-raisers this winter. The one raising money for the orthopedics center, I think." That, at least, wasn't a lie. They had met there. They just hadn't started dating. "He works with medical equipment. He can tell you more about all that. Anyway, we hit it off and he asked me to dinner. Things have just sort of progressed from there."

"Wait," Violet said, sitting at attention on the sofa. "We were all at that fund-raiser. Do we know him? Sebastian who?"

"Sebastian West." Harper was suddenly nervous that maybe they did know him. She and Sebastian hadn't gotten together to talk yet, so she ran the risk of getting caught not knowing something obvious about him if any of the girls knew who he was. Quentin had recognized his name and company, so it was a possibility.

Thankfully none of them perked up at hearing his full name. "I doubt any of you know him. He spends more time working than socializing. He's super smart. I'm excited for you all to meet him." She grinned wide and hoped she was selling her story.

"We're all excited," Violet echoed as her eyes narrowed at Harper in suspicion. "I can't wait for Monday."

Harper took a large sip of her wine and nodded with feigned enthusiasm. "Me neither."

Three

Sunday evening Sebastian arrived at the bar a full fifteen minutes before he was supposed to meet Harper. He wasn't particularly anxious about their meeting, but he couldn't stand just sitting around his apartment any longer. He'd sat there for the last two days trying to fill the hours. Without work, he found he had far too many minutes on his hands.

He'd spent as long as he could packing and preparing for the trip. He'd taken his clothes and his tuxedo to the cleaner. He'd carefully collected his toiletries and underthings, but that had taken only a few hours out of his newfound free time.

Sebastian had tried reading a book. He'd watched some television. Both had bored him after a short while. By Sunday afternoon he'd had nothing to do but pace around his apartment and wish away the hours. He wasn't sure how he'd get through the next two weeks if he hadn't met Harper and had this trip to Ireland fall into his lap. He might just go insane. How was that supposed to improve his health? Mentally weak but physically strong? What good was that?

When his watch showed it was almost time to meet Harper, he'd rushed out the door. He'd taken a table in a quiet corner, ordered himself a gin and tonic with lime—ignoring doctor's orders—and awaited her arrival with his notebook open to read over some notes. He carried it almost everywhere he went, writing down ideas and schematics when they popped into his head. He'd learned the hard way that he could lose the spark of inspiration if he didn't immediately capture it.

This way he was still waiting, but at least he was out of the house and potentially doing something productive in the meantime. Thankfully, Harper showed up a few minutes later. She was looking attractive and fashionable once again with layered lace tops and a long sweater over skinny jeans. Today her dark hair was pulled up into a bun, highlighting the line of her neck and her dangly earrings.

Sebastian was once again struck by the fact that this woman should be able to find a boyfriend easily. He didn't understand why he was even there pretending to be one. Then again, the same thing could probably be said of him. Life was complicated sometimes.

"Thanks for coming. And thanks for doing all of this," she said as she settled into her chair across from him.

"No problem. Would you like a drink?"

"Just water for me," she said with a polite smile. It surprised him. A glass of wine or a martini seemed far more her speed. He didn't question it, however, and waved down the bartender for her water.

"Are you packed and ready to go?" she asked.

"Mostly. What about you?"

"The same. I feel like I'm not ready, although I can't imagine what I haven't packed yet."

"Don't forget the slinky lingerie," Sebastian said. The sudden image of Harper wearing some kind of silk-and-lace chemise came to his mind and made him immediately regret his words. He didn't need that vision haunting him over their next week together.

"What?" Harper's eyes were suddenly wide with concern.

"It was a joke," Sebastian soothed. And that's what he'd intended it to be, even if a part of him wouldn't mind if she threw a nice piece or two in there.

"Oh," she said, visibly relaxing. Apparently the idea of being his girlfriend for real was not nearly as appealing to her as it was in his own mind. "Yeah, no, I'm packing the ugliest pajamas I've got."

"Flannel footie pajamas with a zip front?" he asked.

"Yep. I'll be dressed as a giant pug dog."

Interesting. "Trapdoor for convenience?"

"No, just a front zipper, but they do have a tail and a hood with puppy ears and a nose I can pull up."

"Excellent. Since pugs aren't my thing, I'm sure the sight of you in that dog outfit will squelch any misplaced attraction that might arise between us."

"Perhaps I should buy you one, too. I saw one that was basically a poop emoji costume."

"Not Spider-Man or Deadpool? You went straight for the poop emoji?"

"Yeah, sorry."

They both laughed for a few moments and the tension dissipated between them. Sebastian was relieved. He didn't want either of them to be uncomfortable. It would make the week ten times longer than it would be already.

"So tell me everything I should know about you," Harper began. "I'm your girlfriend, after all, so I need to know all the important things."

Sebastian tried not to wince at the thought of talking about himself. He hated doing that. He tried to think of what he would share with someone if he were really dating them, but he found he didn't know the answer to that, either. "I'm from Maine. A small coastal town called Rockport, specifically. I went to MIT. Technically, I'm a mechanical engineer, but I've branched out quite a bit after college."

"I thought you worked for a medical supply company."

Sebastian frowned. That was probably his fault. He liked to keep the details of his work vague. "Not exactly. BioTech is a medical research and development company. My partner Finn and I develop new medical technology."

"Your partner? You mean you don't just work there?"

"Eh, no. We started the company together out of college. I own it."

Harper frowned, wrinkles creasing her forehead. "Are you serious? I offered you every penny I had in savings to go on this trip and you're the CEO of a company? You probably make more in an afternoon than I do in a paycheck."

Sebastian held up his finger in protest. "You offered me the money. I never said I would actually take it. And I'm not going to, of course."

"So you're rich. Why didn't you say something? Like when Quentin asked about your company?"

At that, Sebastian shrugged. "I'm not the kind to flaunt it. Finn is the face of the company. I'm the mad scientist behind the scenes. I'm happy with the anonymity. I've seen how being well-known and wealthy has complicated his love life and I'm not interested in that."

"In a love life?" Harper asked with an arched brow.

"In a *complicated* love life. Or, hell, maybe a regular one. I work too much for any type of relationship to succeed."

"But you're going to drop everything and go with me on a trip to Ireland on short notice?"

Sebastian sat back in his chair and sighed. It would be easy to tell her that he'd had a heart attack and was on mandatory vacation, but he didn't want to. He didn't like people knowing his business, especially when it changed how they perceived him. Whether it was knowing he was rich, or sick, or used to be poor...it didn't matter. He liked private things to stay private. "When you're the boss, you can do what you want," he responded instead.

She shook her head. "I can't believe you didn't say anything until just now. What if I hadn't asked? Would you have waited until someone recognized you on the plane and I looked like a fool for not knowing my boyfriend is a millionaire?"

"Of course not! I would've told you. And you're one to point fingers, Harper. You're keeping plenty of secrets yourself."

She straightened in her chair and narrowed her gaze at him. "What is that supposed to mean?"

"I saw you walk out of Neiman Marcus with your friends. Then you ditched them and came back ten minutes later to return everything you'd bought. What is that about? It's not buyer's remorse, I'm pretty certain."

Harper's lips twisted in thought as she considered her answer. "I'm trying to save money."

Sebastian looked at her with a pointed expression on his face. There was more to it than just frugality, of that he was sure. He'd done his research since they'd met. Her family owned Orion Computers. She lived in a really nice apartment on the Upper East Side. But she only had two grand in her savings account? That didn't add up in his mind.

His silence prompted her to keep talking. "I'm having a bit of a cash flow shortage. I'm embarrassed about it, so I haven't told anyone, even my friends and family. Until I get things straightened out, I'm trying to be smart about my money, but I have to keep up appearances."

"Like blowing a fortune on designer clothes and then immediately returning them?"

"Yes."

"Don't they notice you never wear them after you buy them?"

She shook her head. "You need a map to get through my closet. Things disappear in there, never to resurface."

Sebastian nodded thoughtfully. "Sounds like a complicated charade to keep up. Pretending to have a boyfriend should be a piece of cake."

"Well, thankfully it's a short-term thing. I should be back on my feet soon and then no one needs to know I lied about it. And as for you and me...well,

I'm sure we will have a sad, but not unexpected, breakup not long after we get back from the trip. Not so soon as to be suspicious, but we can't wait too long or people might start inviting us to things as a couple here in town."

"Sounds tragic. I'm already sad."

Harper looked at him with a smile. "I'm enjoying your sarcastic sense of humor. We might actually be able to pull this off."

"I think so, too. Of course, over time I think you're going to become too clingy for me and we're going to want different things from our relationship."

She groaned. "Ugh. You sound like Quentin. Don't do that or we'll have to just break up now."

Sebastian laughed. "So since we're going to be around that guy, should I know what happened between you two?"

Harper winced at the thought. "That is a story that would require something stronger than water to talk about."

"A cocktail then? My treat," Sebastian added. He waved over the bartender. It wasn't until then that it occurred to him she might be drinking water out of necessity, not desire.

"That's sweet of you. A Cosmo, please."

Once the man returned with the dark pink beverage, Harper took a sip and sighed. "We were together for three years and we've been broken up for two. We met at a party and we really seemed to hit it off.

Things went well between us, but I noticed that it didn't seem to be going anywhere. We'd stalled out at the point where most people take the next step."

"He didn't want anything serious?"

"I thought we were already serious, but I suppose that was my mistake. I was thinking we were on track to get engaged, moving in together…do all the things that other couples around me were doing. But he was always working. Or said he was. He's an attorney and kept insisting he had to put in the long hours if he was going to make partner. I thought it was because he wanted to build a solid future for us, but the truth was that he was perfectly content where we were."

"He was seeing other women."

"Bingo. While I was officially his girlfriend in the public eye, I found out there were three of us he was keeping on the hook. He used long hours at work as his excuse to run around town with different women, and I didn't even question it. I don't know if he couldn't decide and thought that he'd eventually know which one he wanted, or if he just liked keeping that many balls up in the air at once. But eventually I found out about the others and broke it off. When I confronted him, all he said was that he just wasn't ready for a commitment."

Sebastian frowned. "He told you the other day that he's engaged now, didn't he?"

Harper's posture deflated slightly in her chair and he found he hated that. He wanted to punch Quentin in the face for taking such a beautiful, confident woman and leaving her broken.

"Yes," she said softly. "He's bringing her on the trip. You see why I can't go alone? I just can't face him and his fiancée in the state I am in. I'm almost thirty. I'm happy with my life on most days, but I have to admit that I'm not at all where I expected to be at this point. I'm sure everyone else looks at me and thinks I'm the sad, single one in the group."

Sebastian understood. He knew what it was like to be judged by people. While Harper had worked hard to keep up appearances, he'd simply buried his head in his research and tried to block out the rest of the world. It had served him pretty well. Eventually, though, he'd known his avoidance mechanisms would fall apart. His had fallen apart when he'd hit the floor in cardiac arrest. Hers might all come crashing down when her delicately structured pyramid of falsehoods took a hit. He hoped he wouldn't be the reason it fell.

"I will strive to be the imaginary boyfriend you've always dreamed of having someday."

"You go up first," Sebastian said as they stood on the tarmac together. "I prefer to sit in the aisle seat if you don't mind."

Harper nodded and climbed the steps ahead of him to board the private plane. The minute she stepped on and turned the corner, she realized the Boeing Business Jet that Violet's father, Loukas Niarchos, had chartered for the flight wasn't going to be like any plane she'd been on before. Instead of a first-class cabin, she found herself walking through a lounge with a bar, seating areas with couches and swivel chairs, flat-panel televisions and a variety of tables. To the left there was a doorway leading to an executive office where she could see Loukas already chatting on the phone, his laptop open.

A flight attendant greeted them with a smile and directed them through the lounge into the next room to the right. There they found what could be either a conference room or a dining table that sat twenty for a meal. Each chair was plush camel-colored leather with a seat belt if it was necessary. Harper got the feeling the kind of people who chartered flights on this plane wouldn't tolerate turbulence.

"This is like being on Air Force One," Sebastian muttered into her ear as they walked through a narrow hallway past a fully appointed bedroom suite, two full-size bathrooms with showers, and a galley kitchen currently manned by two more smiling flight attendants. "Is this how you're used to traveling?"

Harper shook her head. "No. I'm used to boring old first class unless I'm traveling with family on the Orion corporate jet. That's nice, but it only seats eight. And there's no bedroom. Or office. Or cocktail lounge. My family is normal rich, not filthy rich."

Sebastian chuckled and nudged her forward.

"Good. I don't think I could handle a filthy-rich girl-friend. I'm glad this is a first for us both."

At that point, the plane finally opened up into a traditional seating area. Appointed like a large, first-class cabin, there were six seats in each row. They were in sets of two, divided by two wide aisles. Each seat had its own television screen, blanket, pillow, and controls that allowed its occupant to lay fully flat for sleeping on the overnight flight. A flute of champagne and a chocolate-covered strawberry stenciled with the letters *V&A* in edible gold awaited each guest at their seat as well as a handwritten card in calligraphy with each person's name.

Violet was certainly out to throw a memorable wedding, if nothing else.

They'd been assigned row thirteen of sixteen, seats A and B, so she made her way down the right aisle through the crowd of familiar faces. They were nearly the last to board, so the area was bustling with activity as guests settled in. Quentin hadn't been kidding when he'd said this wedding was the event of the year. People salivated over the idea of receiving a coveted invitation, but the guest list had been kept down to less than a hundred by virtue of the plane and the wedding venue.

Even then, Harper still knew almost everyone on the plane. A few friends and family of Violet's fiancé, Aidan, were unfamiliar to her, but there were far more of Violet's circle than anyone. She smiled and waved politely as she pressed on, even when she saw Quentin in the back row on the far left. He was sitting beside an attractive brunette who seemed a little young for him, but Harper was trying not to let her bitterness color her opinion.

"Here we go," she said as she stopped at their row. Emma and Jonah were seated across the aisle from them in the center section, and Harper could see Emma was already heavily appraising Sebastian from her seat. She tried not to focus on that, instead stowing her bag and her coat in the overhead bin to clear the aisle for others to board.

"Introductions!" Emma said before Harper could even slide into the row to sit.

She pasted on a bright smile and turned their way. "Sebastian, these are my good friends Jonah and Emma Flynn. I work for Jonah's gaming software company, FlynnSoft. You guys, this is my boyfriend, Sebastian West."

Jonah stuck out his hand and the two men exchanged a firm handshake. "Good to meet you both," Sebastian said. "Harper has told me how much she enjoys her job at FlynnSoft. I'm sure that reflects well on you, Jonah."

She tried not to look impressed and instead turned toward her seat. It wasn't until that moment that she noticed a small, white envelope on the window seat. She picked the envelope up and settled in so Sebastian could take his place at her side. She looked around, wondering who might've put it on her seat, but no one seemed to be looking or paying any attention to her. There weren't envelopes like this one on the other seats. Just one for her, with her name written on the front in nondescript block letters.

While Sebastian put his bag in the overhead bin, Harper opened the envelope and pulled out the single page inside. It was handwritten, and relatively short, but it delivered a huge impact.

I know your little secret. If you don't want everyone to find out the truth and risk your big inheritance, you'll do exactly what I say. Once we arrive in Ireland, you'll go to the bank and withdraw a hundred thousand dollars. Then you'll leave it in an envelope at the front desk of the hotel for "B. Mayler" by dinnertime tomorrow. Miss the deadline and I'm going to make a big problem for you, Harper.

She read the words a dozen times, trying to make sense of it all, but there was no way to make sense of what she was seeing. Her heart was pounding in her ears, deafening her to anything but the sound of her internal panic. The fantastic plane and everyone on it faded into the background.

This was blackmail. She was being blackmailed.

How was that even possible?

Harper had been so careful about her secret. Aside from sharing some of it with Sebastian yesterday, no one, not her closest friends or family, knew the truth. Not even her brother or father knew about her financial difficulties. She'd kept it quiet for over eight years, working hard to make ends meet until the next payment came and she didn't have to fake it any longer. Sebastian had been the first to question her curious behavior, and it hadn't seemed to hurt to share a little information with him considering her birthday was right around the corner.

But someone had found out her secret, and that was a big problem.

Her grandfather on her mother's side of the family had set up a thirty-million-dollar trust fund for both her and her brother when they were born. It included a two-million-dollar payment on their eighteenth birthdays followed by a twenty-eight-million-dollar payment on their thirtieth birthdays. Harper's thirtieth was only a few weeks away now. She could see the light at the end of the tunnel. She should be coasting to the finish line, but her foolish youthful behavior had put everything at risk.

After her father ran into financial troubles with his gold-digging second wife, her grandfather had added a new provision to the grandchildren's trusts—if it was discovered that they had been financially irresponsible with their first payments, there would be no second payment. Ever-responsible Oliver had had no problem managing his money and had made his own fortune many times over. He hardly needed the second payment by the time his thirtieth birthday came around. But not Harper. By the time the provision was added, her frivolous lifestyle had already helped her blow through most of the first two million.

When she found out about the addendum, she'd realized she had to keep her situation a secret. Her grandfather couldn't find out or she'd risk the money she desperately needed. That second payment would put an end to her charade. She wouldn't have to eat ramen noodles for weeks to pay her massive building fee at the beginning of the year. She wouldn't have to return everything she bought and scour the thrift stores for designer finds to keep up her facade of a spoiled heiress. Harper wouldn't blow this new money—she wasn't a naive child any longer—but it would be nice not to have to pretend she had more than two grand in her savings account.

Thankfully that two thousand dollars she'd earmarked for Sebastian could stay put. It was all she had aside from her FlynnSoft 401K with its stiff withdrawal penalties. Where was she going to come up with a hundred thousand dollars by tomorrow? In a month, easy. But now…it was an impossible task.

"Are you okay?"

Harper quickly folded the letter closed and shoved it back into the envelope. She looked over at Sebastian, who had settled into his seat and buckled up. "I'm fine," she said. "Just reading over something."

"You look like the plane is about to crash," he

noted. "You're white as a sheet. Since they haven't even closed the cabin door yet, I was concerned."

"Flying isn't my favorite thing," she lied, and slipped the note into her purse. "Even on a fancy jet like this. My doctor gave me some pills and I hope to wake up in Ireland before I know it."

"Sleep? And miss a minute of this luxurious travel?" Sebastian picked up his crystal champagne flute. "Shall we toast before you slip into a drug-induced coma?"

Harper picked up her drink and fought to keep her hand from trembling with nerves. "What should we drink to?"

"To a safe, fun and *romantic* trip," he suggested with a knowing smile.

"I'll drink to that." She gently clinked her glass to his and downed the entire flute in one nervous gulp. Sebastian arched a curious eyebrow at her, but she ignored him. She needed some alcohol, stat, before that note sent her into hysterics.

Turning away from him, she fastened her seat belt, sat back and closed her eyes.

"You'll be fine," he soothed. "You're surrounded by friends and family. I'm here to hold your hand through the whole flight if you need me to. You don't have a thing to worry about."

Normally he would be right, and if her nerves were over flying, it might be helpful. But she couldn't feel safe and relax knowing that one of the people on this plane—one of her very own friends and family—was her blackmailer.

This was going to be a long trip.

Four

"What a great room!"

Harper followed Sebastian into their room at the hotel, grateful to finally be there. The flight itself had been uneventful once they'd taken off. She'd taken the pills with another glass of champagne—probably not the best idea—and woken when the wheels touched down in Dublin. Even if she'd had the money to pay her blackmailer, she hadn't had the chance to stop at a bank and get it. Two chartered luxury buses had picked them up at the airport and transported everyone on the nearly three-hour drive through the Irish countryside to their final destination of Markree Castle. The castle and its sprawling grounds had been renovated into a hotel and the entire location had been rented to house their group and host the wedding and reception.

Sebastian had looked out the window on the bus, contentedly taking in the lush green landscape as it went by, but Harper hadn't been able to enjoy it. Every person who'd passed by her was run through a mental checklist of potential guilt or innocence. She supposed that was the most unnerving part of it all. This wasn't just some random internet criminal who'd dug up some dirt and tried to make a dime off her. It was someone she knew. Someone she trusted. She couldn't quite wrap her head around that.

Like she didn't already have enough to worry about on this trip. She eyeballed Sebastian as he sat on the bed and gave it a test bounce. It wasn't a large bed—a double perhaps—which would mean close quarters at night. Harper hadn't thought much about that when she'd concocted this plan. A lot of hotels in Europe had twin beds and that was what she'd expected. Just her luck that they'd end up with a room obviously appointed for lovers. Lovers who wanted to be close all the time.

She'd have to thank Violet for hooking her up, she thought drily.

The room was small but well done. There were towels twisted into swans in the bathroom, rose-scented bubble bath on the edge of the claw-foot tub, candles, lace curtains, red foil-wrapped heart chocolates on their pillows, a velvet love seat by the fireplace… Were this any other trip with any other man, Harper would be thrilled with the romantic vibe. It might help set the mood for their romantic ruse, but at the moment, pretending to have a boyfriend seemed pretty unimportant. Now she wished her only problem was being single.

As it was, it felt like the universe was just screwing with her.

"What's wrong with you?"

Harper turned toward Sebastian with a frown. "What do you mean?"

He watched her, stroking his dark goatee with thought. "I mean, you've been acting funny since we got on the plane to come here. I thought it was nerves, but it's been hours since we landed and you seem as distant as ever. We're in Ireland. Everyone thinks we're an adorable couple. You should be happy. What's going on?"

It was just her luck that her fake boyfriend would be so in tune with her emotions. Quentin wouldn't have noticed, but he was rarely concerned with anything but himself. She opened her mouth to tell him that she was fine, but his movement stopped her.

Getting up from the bed, he crossed the room and stood directly in front of her. He was close enough to reach out and touch. It took everything she had not to fall into his arms and let his strong embrace protect her from the outside world. But that felt a little too forward for their current situation.

Instead he stood close, without touching, looking deeply into her eyes. "And don't tell me it's nothing," he added. "My mother carried the weight of the world on her shoulders but would always insist that everything was fine. It was something then and it's something now. I know it when I see it."

Harper wanted to tell him. She needed to tell someone. Maybe he would know what to do, because she sure as hell didn't know how to handle this situation. She'd never been blackmailed before. Pulling away from him, she grabbed her purse off the entryway table and withdrew the small envelope from inside it. She handed it to Sebastian without a single word of explanation.

Sebastian's gaze flickered quickly over the note. By the time he was finished, his mouth had fallen into a deep frown of displeasure. Combined with his dark hair and eyes, something about his usual easygoing demeanor seemed to shift to almost wicked. Like she'd angered Bruce Banner. She almost expected his eyes to glow red with fury when he looked up at her. Instead she found them unexpectedly soft with concern. He was irate, but not with her.

"Where did this come from?" he asked, holding the note up.

"It was on my seat when we got on the plane. That's all I know." Harper wrapped her sweater tighter around her, as though it would help. She wished she had something more to go on, but she didn't. It was on generic white stationery and written with a block print text that anyone could do. There was nothing to give any kind of hint about who had left it there.

"Why didn't you say something to me?" he asked.

"When? When we were trapped on a plane for eight hours with eighty other people—one of whom was probably the blackmailer? They were likely watching me, waiting for my reaction to finding their little love note. So I didn't give them the satisfaction of panicking. I took my pills and went to sleep like it was nothing. But it's not nothing. I'm worried sick about this whole thing. Thankfully you're the only one to notice."

Sebastian looked over the note again before handing it back to her. His mouth tightened with irritation, highlighting the sharp, square lines of his jaw and the dark goatee that framed it. "So you suspect it's one of the wedding guests? Not the flight crew?"

Harper shrugged and tore her gaze from the tempting curve of his bottom lip. She wanted more than anything to focus on that. To lose herself in Sebastian's kiss and forget about the mess she was in. She got the feeling he wouldn't mind indulging her with a little distraction. But this wasn't the time. Blackmail was serious business.

"I'd never seen any of the crew before. We were one of the last couples to board, so almost any of the guests could've put it on my seat. As you've read, I'm supposed to leave the money at the front desk, so it has to be someone that's still here in Sligo with us. I'm sure the flight crew is back in Dublin."

She sank onto the bed, clutching the note in her hand. Where she hadn't allowed herself to really react on the flight, now, in the privacy of their hotel suite, she felt herself starting to emotionally unravel. "What am I going to do, Sebastian?" she asked with eyes squeezed tightly shut to trap the tears. She hated to cry.

She felt the bed sag beside her and Sebastian's comforting warmth against her side. "The way I see it, you've got three options. One, you pay the blackmail. That will keep your secret under wraps, but you're giving the blackmailer the upper hand. I don't know what you're being blackmailed for, but at any time they could demand more money to stay quiet. You'll never really be free of the blackmailer's hold on your life. But that's a risk that might be worth taking. Only you can answer that question."

She knew paying the blackmailer wasn't the best choice, but it was the one she'd take if given the chance. Unfortunately that wasn't an option for her. "I couldn't pay it even if I wanted to. I told you before that I was in a tight spot financially. It's possible that given some time I could go to a bank and get a loan with my apartment for collateral. But they want it tonight. By dinnertime. That's just impossible, especially considering we're in the middle of a remote estate in the Irish countryside. Even in Dublin, I couldn't have pulled it off."

"Okay," Sebastian said after listening to her logic. "The second option would be to call the police. Blackmail is illegal. They could take prints off the card, perhaps leave a dummy package at the desk for the culprit to pick up and then arrest them. You'll run the risk of the secret being exposed in the process, but they'll get their punishment."

Harper shook her head. She didn't want cops involved. Not in this situation. It would be bad enough for her to lose her inheritance and for everyone to find out what she'd done. She didn't need her story being in the newspapers, too.

"What's option three?" she asked.

"Option three is to expose the secret yourself and take their power away."

She could do that, but it would be a twenty-eight-million-dollar decision. Just the thought made her stomach start to ache with dread. She was stuck between a rock and a hard place. "I… I can't. It will ruin everything I've worked so hard to achieve."

Harper felt Sebastian's arm wrap around her shoulders. She couldn't resist leaning into him and resting her head against his chest. It was soothing to listen to the beating of his heart and enjoy the warmth of his embrace. It had been a long time since she'd had someone in her life to hold her like this. To listen to her when she had worries on her mind. She knew she had been lonely, but she didn't realize how deeply she'd felt it until this moment.

"Harper," Sebastian said after a long silence with her in his arms. "I have to ask this. Whether or not you answer is up to you, but it's hard for me to help you when I don't know. What could you have done to be blackmailed for?"

She knew the question would come eventually. Harper dreaded having to explain her youthful stupidity to anyone, but for some reason it was worse to tell Sebastian. He was successful, like her brother. He never would've made the mistakes she'd made. But she needed to tell someone. To have one person on this trip she could trust. He was the only one she could eliminate as a suspect since he couldn't possibly have left the note on her seat.

Harper sighed heavily and buried her face into his chest to avoid speaking for a little while longer. She pressed her nose to his collar and breathed in the spicy scent of his cologne and his skin. It was easy to stay there and pretend that everything would be okay for a little while longer.

"I'm a spoiled little rich girl," she said at last.

"Tell me something I don't know," Sebastian responded unexpectedly.

Harper sat up sharply and frowned at him.

"I'm kidding," he said. "Please continue. I'm just trying to keep things light."

Harper slumped over and sighed. "My brother and

I originally had trust funds set up for thirty million dollars each. When my mother died, my grandfather decided that, without her guidance, it might be better to break it into two payments. A small, two-million-dollar payment when we turned eighteen, followed by the rest when we turned thirty."

"Makes sense. An eighteen-year-old is more likely to blow all the money and have nothing to show for it."

"Exactly. And, basically, that's what I did. My father had given me everything I could ever want. When I went off to college, I continued to live that way, just on my own money for a change. When I started to run low, my father pitched in. But then he ran into his own financial problems and I was on my own."

"I don't hear anything that's blackmail worthy. Did you spend all the money on drugs or something?"

"Of course not! I spent it on shoes. Clothes. Trips. Makeup. Designer handbags. Expensive meals. Nonsense, really, but what I'd always been used to. And, no, nothing was criminal. Embarrassing, but not criminal. I went to Yale for a finance degree and yet I was a fool with my own money. No…the problem came after my father got a divorce. My grandfather was worried that our dad had set a bad example and added an additional requirement to the trust to keep us in line—if we blew the first payment, we wouldn't get the second."

"Does he know what you did?" Sebastian asked.

"No. Most of the money was long gone before he even added the stipulation, but I'd transferred the funds into my private accounts so no one had any insight into my finances. But someone has found out. And if I can't magically come up with a hundred grand, it's going to cost me a cool twenty-eight million instead."

Sebastian's blood was boiling. He was pretty sure his doctor wouldn't be too pleased that his relaxing vacation time had been overshadowed by drama of the worst kind. He could hear his pulse pounding in his ears as he marched down the stone hallway of the castle.

Harper was still in their room, spinning in circles and attempting to unpack her luggage. He'd stepped out to give her some privacy and to get a little air. The truth was that he didn't want her to know how angry he was over her whole situation. After her confession, she might mistakenly think he was angry with her and he was anything but.

Instead he was feeling remarkably protective of Harper. It was almost as though she really was his girlfriend. With her curled up in his arms, it was hard for him to remember this was all a sham. It certainly felt real. Maybe too real for the first day of the charade.

Before he'd left the room, he'd promised to keep

her secret, with one caveat. If he found out who her blackmailer was before she did, he couldn't promise her that he wouldn't cause some trouble for the jerk. She might not know that Sebastian had grown up on the wrong side of the tracks, but he had and, at a moment's notice, the scrappy kid who'd used his fists to defend himself could come out. Whomever was putting Harper through this hell deserved a black eye. Or two.

Even as Sebastian headed down the staircase to the main lobby, he could feel his hands curl into tight fists. He was strung tight, clutching his notebook under his arm and ready to fight at the slightest provocation. He hadn't been sure where he was going when he'd left the room, but he found himself loitering around the front desk. Perhaps the culprit would be there, waiting on a payment to be dropped off.

He was in no mindset to work, so he set aside his notebook, grabbed a copy of the local paper and settled into a large wingback chair by the fireplace. Despite being early summer, it was Ireland and that still meant cool weather, especially given they were near the northwest coast. The fire offered a comfortable, draft-free place to sit in the stone behemoth of a building.

Sebastian glanced over the words in the paper, but he was focused more on the comings and goings. There were few at this hour of the afternoon. It was likely that many had fallen prey to jet lag and were napping in their rooms before the welcome dinner. Most of the people he saw in the lobby were wearing the uniforms of the hotel staff.

After about thirty minutes, out of the corner of his eye, he noticed someone approach the front desk. He turned his attention fully to the man standing there, realizing almost immediately that it was one of the few people on the trip he actually knew—Harper's ex, Quentin.

That made sense. Harper had mentioned that she'd been short on cash basically since college and she'd only dated Quentin a few years ago. If they'd been at all serious, there had to have been signs of her difficulties. Sebastian had noticed it in minutes. Quentin, of all people, should have been able to tell if Harper was broke. If not, maybe she'd confided in him and forgotten about it. And perhaps he might also know that her financial luck was about to change. It made sense. But would he be bold enough to try to get a piece of it?

Quentin stood nervously waiting at the counter for the desk clerk to return and, after a brief exchange Sebastian couldn't hear, turned and headed back toward the elevators empty-handed. He glanced around the lobby as he walked, an almost agitated expression lining his face. And then his gaze met with Sebastian's pointed glare.

He knew he could turn away. Try to appear more subtle in his appraisal. But at the moment, Sebastian didn't care if the bastard knew he was watching him. Let him know they were on to his sick game. Let him check the desk twenty times tonight. He was going to be disappointed. No matter what Harper wanted to do, she was right about one thing. There wasn't going to be any way to pull a hundred grand out of thin air in a foreign country.

It might even be a tricky thing for Sebastian to do and he had ten times that much cash in his checking account at any given time. Banks simply didn't like handing over that much money. There were too many checks and balances, wire transfers, international calls and such before they parted with it. Perhaps if they were in Monte Carlo where people parted with larger amounts in the casinos on a regular basis, but rural Ireland? Not likely. If Quentin was behind this blackmail plot, his timing was crappy.

Quentin quickly broke their connection with an anxious biting of his lip and turned his back to wait for the elevator. Within a few seconds it opened and he disappeared without looking back in Sebastian's direction.

Sebastian was so engrossed in watching his mark that he didn't notice someone approaching his chair.

"May I join you?"

He turned and recognized Harper's older brother standing there. Oliver and his wife, Lucy, had been introduced briefly to him on the bus, but they really hadn't had time to talk aside from some basic pleasantries. Sebastian expected that he had questions for the new boyfriend. Any brother worth his salt would when his little sister was involved, even if she was a grown woman. "Please, have a seat. I'm just trying to stay awake until dinnertime, so I could use some company."

Oliver chuckled and settled into the other wingback chair. He had a cut-crystal lowball glass in his hand filled with some ice and a dark amber liquor. "I know how that is. International travel messes with your internal clock. I'm hoping to eat a huge dinner, have a couple drinks and pass out at a reasonable hour. Whatever that is. I'm not sure if Harper told you, but Lucy and I have nine-month-old twins. Our sleep schedules haven't been reasonable in quite some time."

"I can imagine. I wouldn't be surprised if the two of you did nothing but sleep when a wedding event wasn't taking place." Sebastian hadn't noticed any children on the flight but Violet and Aidan's toddler, so he presumed they were all back in New York with their nannies and their grandparents. Sounded like the perfect getaway to relax, nap and have some alone time together.

And yet he was downstairs with Sebastian instead.

"Lucy is actually napping right now. I told her not to because it would screw up her sleep, but she told me to mind my own business and go downstairs." Oliver chuckled and sipped at his drink. "They're a sassy group of women, my sister included. I never thought I'd be roped into all of it, and yet here I am. Do you know what you're getting yourself into, Sebastian?"

He smiled. He was pretty sure he was in over his head when he'd agreed to go on this trip and she'd kissed him in the department store. "If I didn't, I'm getting a good feel for it on this trip," he said. "It's been quite the experience so far and it's only the first day here. Being the odd man out allows me to sort of observe from the fringes, which is fine by me. To be honest, I don't spend a lot of time with people. Certainly not like this. My business partner, Finn Solomon, is the outward face of our company. I spend most of my time sketching out plans or tinkering with my latest ideas in the lab at work."

"I used to be that way. When I inherited Orion from my father, the company was a mess. Apple was king and PCs weren't cool anymore. Especially those old tower dinosaurs everyone had at work or in their closets. I sacrificed a lot of my personal life sitting with my engineers, trying to brainstorm new computer products that would make us competitive again. Now, of course, we're back on our feet and I'm able to shift my focus to other more important things, like Lucy and the twins. Say, have you been married before?"

Let the prying begin. Nice segue. "I haven't. I suppose I've been more focused on building our company, so I've never married or had any children."

Oliver nodded thoughtfully. "You know, all of Harper's friends have recently settled down and had children. After Violet and Aidan get married this weekend, Harper will be the only single one left."

"She's mentioned that."

"I suppose she feels some pressure to follow suit."

Sebastian narrowed his gaze at Oliver. "You're asking if Harper is barking up the wrong tree with me since I'm a thirty-eight-year-old workaholic bachelor?"

Oliver simply shrugged and sipped his drink. "Is she?"

"I suppose I'm getting to the age where I need to take the idea of a family more seriously, but until Harper, it hadn't really crossed my mind. I'm not opposed to it, no, but it simply hasn't been in the cards for me yet."

Her brother listened thoughtfully and nodded. "I was the same way until Lucy blew through my life like a hurricane. I didn't think I was ready for marriage or children, either, but she changed everything. It was like my eyes were suddenly opened and all I could see was her and our future together. Is it like that with you and my sister?"

That was something Sebastian didn't think he could lie about. It was easy to pretend to date and to be attracted to Harper because he was attracted to her. But to love her? To envision their future together? That was different and he had no doubt her brother could spot it if he fibbed. "It's only been a few months, but I think we're definitely getting to a more serious place. I care for your sister," he said.

And he did. He didn't want to see her get hurt, be it by him or Quentin or whomever that sleazy blackmailer was. That meant he cared a little, even for a woman he hardly knew. It was hard not to when he'd been drawn into her world and her problems so quickly. If Lucy was a hurricane, perhaps Harper was a tornado, plucking him from a wheat field and sucking him up into the swirling drama of her life.

"Listen, I don't want to do that stereotypical brother thing where I threaten you not to hurt my sister and wave around my shotgun. It's kind of cliché and not that effective, if Quentin is any evidence of that. I also don't own a shotgun. But I will say that you're the first man my sister has seriously dated in quite a while. I'm happy for you both, but I'm also nervous. She's kept this relationship quiet and the fact that she's suddenly announcing it to the world means she's feeling more comfortable with her feelings for you, whatever they may be. My sister is all sarcasm and sass on the outside, but all that is there as a barrier to protect the fact that she's really a marshmallow on the inside. She gets hurt easily."

Sebastian listened carefully. Even though he knew this relationship wasn't real, he took her brother's words to heart. He'd already been a witness to Harper's softer side—the side that was nervous about what other people thought of her and the part that was tied in knots over her secrets being exposed. She definitely had a soft underbelly. To be honest, seeing that part of her had endeared her to him more than he realized. She wasn't just the snarky single friend living the footloose and fancy-free life in Manhattan. She was more than that. Much more. And it made Sebastian curious to unearth more of her hidden layers.

Oliver glanced down at his watch and sighed before finishing off his drink. "Well, I'm glad we could have this little chat. I'd better head upstairs and wake Lucy so she has time to freshen up before dinner. I'll see you and Harper there in a little while."

"We'll see you later," Sebastian said with a wave. He watched Oliver disappear from the lobby and glanced back over at the hotel front desk. He hadn't been watching it for at least fifteen or twenty minutes. Anyone looking for the package of blackmail money could've come and gone and he'd missed it while chatting with Oliver.

Frustrated, he folded up the newspaper and decided to follow Oliver's suit. It was almost time for the welcome dinner in the great hall and he could use some time to change. With a sigh, he picked up his notebook and headed for the staircase to find Harper to report on what he'd seen, carefully leaving out her brother's little chat.

As far as he was concerned, Quentin should be at the top of the suspect list and he was going to keep an eye on him.

Five

Since everyone was tired, the welcome dinner was short and, for that, Harper was relieved. Aidan and Violet said a few words, thanked everyone for coming, and every couple was given a gift bag. Inside were some useful essentials: a schedule of activities, a map of the property and some authentic Irish chocolates.

Harper had difficulty focusing on any of the food or conversation. Her eyes kept running over each guest, wondering which one was expecting to be a hundred grand richer before bedtime. No one was watching her, no one was acting odd, and yet she could feel someone's eyes on her. Her gaze flicked over to Quentin. He seemed a little out of sorts tonight. He fidgeted with his food and didn't engage anyone, even his fiancée, in conversation.

After Sebastian had mentioned seeing her ex go by the front desk, it had confirmed her suspicions that he might be behind this. He was the only one who made sense. He knew a little about her situation, or he had back when they dated. The question was whether or not he needed money badly enough to use it against her. She didn't know. A hundred grand wasn't a lot in the scheme of things. All she knew was that she hated being in the same room with him. She wanted to escape upstairs as soon as she could.

At the same time, as they got up to leave the great hall, Harper realized she was also dreading going back to the suite with Sebastian. When he'd returned to the room before dinner, she had thankfully already dressed for the evening. She'd been in the process of curling her hair in the bathroom as he'd entered their room. He'd gone about changing his clothes, paying no attention to the fact that Harper was in the next room with the door wide open.

She'd tried not to stare in the mirror at him as he'd walked around in his navy boxer briefs, laying out his outfit. She'd told herself that it was surprise, not desire, that had caused her to study his mostly naked body so closely. She'd expected the mad scientist to be soft through the middle from long hours at the lab and less-than-ideal eating habits, but he wasn't. His body was long and lean with hard muscles that twitched beneath tanned skin that extended far below his collar line.

How did he get a body like that working in his lab for long stretches of time?

"Ye-ouch!" she'd hollered, pulling her attention back to the blazing-hot curling iron where it belonged. She'd sucked at her burned finger and focused on finishing her hair, even when he'd come into the bathroom still in his underwear. He'd bent over the sink to splash water on his face and beard, then combed his hair back and was done. Men had it so easy.

"Could you put on a robe or something?" she'd finally asked. Despite her best intentions to ignore him when they were alone, she was sure to burn off a chunk of hair if he kept walking around mostly naked.

Sebastian had seemed startled and mildly insulted by the request at first, but had quickly retrieved one of the resort robes and covered up.

She'd thanked him and the tension between them eased. They'd finished dressing, gone down to the great hall and sat together throughout the meal, engaging in polite conversation with those around them. They'd smiled, leaned into each other, shared bites of food and were as lovey-dovey as they could stand to be until they were finally released for some welcome rest.

Now that she'd had an eyeful of what he was hiding under his suits, Harper wasn't sure how well she would sleep tonight. Not lying a mere inch or two from Sebastian for hours on end.

They bypassed the elevator and walked slowly and silently up the staircase together to their suite. About halfway up, Harper felt the brush of Sebastian's fingers against her own. She looked down and put her hand in his when she realized he was intentionally reaching for her. He was right. They should be holding hands. She couldn't let any awkwardness that happened behind closed doors impact the show they were putting on for everyone else.

If only touching him didn't unnerve her the way it did. His hand was large and warm, enveloping hers in a way that made heat radiate up her arm. By the time they reached their room, her blood was humming through her veins and she felt as if the silk pussy bow that tied at the collar of the Fendi blouse she'd chosen was about to choke her. She also felt flush in the otherwise cool castle. That could only be Sebastian's doing.

He let go of her hand long enough to open the door and let her step in ahead of him. He followed behind, pulling the door shut and fastening the privacy latch.

Harper wasn't the only one who was oddly overheated. As she untied the bow at her neck, she watched Sebastian slip quickly out of his suitcoat and tug his tie loose. She found her eyes drawn to the hollow of his throat as he unfastened his collar and continued down the line of buttons until a touch of dark chest hair was exposed.

Suddenly the thought of pressing a kiss against that part of his neck appeared in her mind. The warm scent of his skin, the stubble brushing her cheeks, the rhythmic thump of his pulse against her lips… An unwelcome tingle of desire surged through her whole body, making her belly clench and her breasts ache with longing in the confines of her bra.

When her nervous gaze met his, she found a questioning look in his eyes and a room that was abruptly very quiet. "What?" she asked before turning away to focus on kicking out of her pointy-toed heels.

Sebastian just shrugged and sat in a chair to pull off his shoes. "You were staring at me, that's all. I was waiting for you to say something. Did I get some shepherd's pie on my shirt?" He looked down at the pristine gray shirt.

She wished he was a mess. Maybe then she could ignore the building attraction between them. Instead, he'd been the perfect companion so far. Perfect aside from being too attractive, too nice and too supportive. A soft, pasty midsection would really help her control her libido right now, but she knew that what was under that shirt was anything but. "No. I just… got lost in my thoughts, I guess."

It was then that, with them both in states of partial dress, they found themselves at an impasse. Harper didn't know what to do next. She certainly wasn't about to tell him what was on her mind. If she stood there any longer, he'd continue to undress like before. She supposed she could gather up her pajamas and take them into the bathroom to change like this was a sleepover with a group of shy ten-year-old girls. Perhaps that would give him time to change privately, as well.

She turned to where her luggage was sitting open and started riffling through it. Thankfully she'd thought to pack pajamas that were less than intriguing. She had passed on the dog onesie—it was too bulky—but had chosen something just as unappealing. There was a piece of nice lingerie for show, but the rest was purely practical in nature. They were flannel, for the potentially cold Irish nights, and long-sleeved, to keep any glimpses of exposed skin to a minimum.

"Here," he said.

Harper turned her attention to Sebastian in time to see him deliberately taking off the rest of his clothes. "Um, what are you doing?" she asked, clutching her pajamas to her breasts for dear life as she realized what was happening.

"I'm getting this out of the way." He shrugged off his dress shirt and stepped out of the suit pants that had pooled at his feet. "We can't spend this whole week tiptoeing around each other and if you keep burning fingers on your curling iron while you sneak peeks at me, people are going to start asking questions. We're sharing a room. Sharing a bed. It doesn't matter what does or doesn't happen in the bed—we need to be more comfortable around each other. You said so yourself when we first agreed to this whole thing." Standing in nothing but those same navy boxer briefs, Sebastian held out his arms. "Take a good look. Get it out of your system. It's just the standard equipment."

Harper watched with confusion and curiosity as he displayed himself to her. His equipment was anything but standard. Her gaze flickered from his defined biceps to the chest hair across his pecs to the trail that ran down his stomach to the gray waistband of his briefs. She was tempted to glance lower, but he turned, giving her a look at his muscular back and curved rear end, as well.

"Well?" he asked with his back to her.

"Why are you so tanned?" she blurted out to her own embarrassment.

He turned around to face her with a smile. "You're staring at my ass but your only question is why I'm tanned?" He shrugged, unfazed by her question. "Okay, well, my apartment building has a rooftop pool. I swim a lot. It's one of my stress relievers. It's not enough, apparently, but it's what I do. I'm not big on going to the gym. It's boring."

"What do you mean it's not enough?"

Sebastian's lips twisted for a moment in thought and he shook his head. "Nothing. There's not enough stress relievers in the world when you're in my line of work, that's all." He looked down at his chest and back at her. "Seen enough?"

Harper nodded nervously.

Sebastian mirrored her nod and sought out a pair of lounging pants from his bag. He tugged them on and looked at her with a wry grin. "Now when you talk to your girlfriends about getting me out of my pants, you don't have to lie."

Harper smiled, still fiercely holding her pajamas as though they were a protective armor. It felt silly after that to hide in the bathroom to change, but was she brave enough to do it out here?

"Your turn."

Her gaze met his. "What?" she said with obvious panic in her voice. Did he honestly expect her to parade around mostly naked because he had?

He held up his hands to deflect the blowback. "I'm just kidding Harper. Relax."

Harper held in a nervous twitter of laughter at his joke. "Oh."

"It's nothing I haven't seen before, anyway," he added. "I'm sure it's nice and all, but I'm not about to hurt myself while I stare at you."

Harper didn't know if she should be relieved or offended. He'd told her before that she was beautiful, but at the moment he seemed as though he couldn't care less about catching a glimpse of her naked body. Maybe he was using reverse psychology on her, she couldn't be sure, but she had the sudden urge to take off her clothes and prove him wrong.

Against her better judgment, she went with the surge of bravery and decided to put him to the test. "That's good to know," she said. She set her pajamas on the edge of the bed and pulled her blouse up over her head. She paid no attention to Sebastian as she straightened the straps of her cream-satin bra and unzipped her pencil skirt. She let it pool to her ankles, bending slowly to pick it up off the floor and to give him all the time he might need to see her cream thong and firm ass. She'd spent a lot of hours in the gym working on that butt and he damn well better be impressed by it.

She wanted to turn and look at him. For some reason, she wanted to see naked desire and need in his eyes. She knew it was there—she could practically feel his gaze on her body. But she didn't dare look at him. She wasn't sure what she would do if she found what she was looking for. Would she act on it? Ignore it? As it was, they would both spend tonight aching for something they couldn't have.

Harper decided not to turn in Sebastian's direction. It was enough to know that he hadn't moved from his spot since she'd started undressing. She forced herself to step into the plaid pajama pants. She unbuttoned the flannel top and readied it to put on before reaching back to unfasten her bra. Before she could slip it from her shoulders, she caught a blur of movement from the corner of her eye and a moment later the bathroom door shut hard. The shower came on not long after that.

So much for being comfortable around each other and getting it out of their system, she thought. Harper continued to put on her pajamas with a grin.

It was only the first day and she could already tell this was going to be a miserably boring trip.

It was not at all what she had envisioned when they'd been invited to the glamorous overseas wedding of Violet Niarchos and Aidan Murphy. Yes, sure, they'd flown on a snazzy chartered plane and were sleeping in a private Irish castle, but watching the Queen of England snore into her teacup would be more exciting than hanging around this rotting pile of bricks with a bunch of blowhard billionaires.

She'd heard the wedding coordinator talking to her assistant on the plane about the week's itinerary. It sounded like one boring event after another with no end in sight. The week promised "highlights" like a round of golf for the gentlemen, a tea party for the ladies and shopping excursions into the sleepy village by the sea.

Couldn't they have at least stayed in Dublin for a night? Every person who walked past her in the hallway was worth a bloody fortune and yet hadn't the slightest clue how to have any fun with their money.

If not for the little blackmail scheme she was running, the whole trip would be a waste of her time. So far, even that had proven fruitless as far as money went, but it had been something to do. Watching Harper squirm under the pressure of blackmail was nice, but it wasn't what she really wanted.

That spoiled little princess needed to shut up and pay up. She could afford it. It was one tiny fraction of the fortune she was set to inherit from her dear old grandfather. Harper hadn't worked for or earned that money. It was to be dropped in her lap just because she'd been born into a family that handed down multi-million-dollar trust funds just as easily as other people passed hazel eyes and freckles down to their children.

She might not have all the money now, but she would have it soon. In the meantime, Harper could easily get her hands on it. She could borrow it from one of her rich friends, her brother...even her new boyfriend was loaded. Basically anyone on that flight could hand over the cash without blinking. Harper just needed the right motivation to ask.

Harper didn't deserve twenty-eight million dollars. She didn't even deserve the twenty-seven million, nine hundred thousand that would be left after she paid the blackmail.

She deserved it. She needed it.

And she was going to get it before the week was up.

That was the longest night of Sebastian's life.

As it was, he'd stayed in the bathroom far longer

than was necessary. After he'd showered and tried to take the edge off, he'd meticulously brushed and flossed his teeth, rinsed with mouthwash, washed his face…anything and everything he could do to kill time and wipe the image of Harper's near naked body from his mind.

She might as well have been naked. That tantalizing little thong left almost nothing to the imagination and with the creamy color that nearly matched her skin, the rest of it just blended away. He'd tried to play it cool. Act like the mature adult he thought he was when they'd started this little game. He'd gritted his teeth, tried to think of the most un-arousing things he could, and even closed his eyes for a moment or two. But he hadn't been able to keep his gaze away for long. When she'd moved to take her bra off, though, he'd known he'd had to go.

It was that or… No. That hadn't been an option.

Theirs was a fake relationship. Despite all the handholding, embraces and canoodling they did in public, it was all fake. They weren't in love. They hardly knew one another. When he'd signed up for this, he'd thought it wouldn't be that hard to pretend to be Harper's lover. Now he wanted it for real so badly he could hardly draw in the scent of her perfume without gaining an erection.

By the time he'd come out of the bathroom, almost all the lights were out and Harper had been in bed. She'd been lying on her side with her back to him, so he'd been able to get into bed, turn off the nearby lamp and go to sleep without having to face her again.

At least that had been the idea. Instead he'd spent most of the night tossing and turning. He'd felt anxious. Squirmy. Filled with nervous energy that he couldn't shake. He should have been exhausted after staying up all day to adjust to the time change, but it hadn't mattered. All Sebastian's body cared about was the warm, soft female lying mere inches from him.

He remembered seeing the light of dawn through the curtains right around the time he was finally able to doze off. The next thing he heard was the shower running. When Harper emerged from the bathroom—fully dressed, thank goodness—she sat in the chair and rifled through the welcome bag they'd received the night before.

"What's on the agenda today?" he muttered into his pillow with a gravelly, sleepy voice.

"Today they've chartered a bus into the nearby town of Sligo if anyone wants to go shop or sightsee. It leaves at ten, after breakfast is done."

"And when is breakfast?"

"About fifteen minutes from now."

Reluctantly, Sebastian pushed himself up and swung his legs out of bed. "I'll be ready in ten," he grumbled as he stumbled into the shower and turned on the water.

He quickly washed his hair and body, cleaned up his goatee, and was ready to go in ten minutes, as he'd predicted. He was wearing a more casual outfit for a day in town, so the jeans and polo shirt had come together quickly. Harper was dressed more casually, as well. When she stood to leave, he couldn't help but notice her skinny jeans were like a second skin. They clung to the delicious curve of her ass and thighs, bringing back flashes from the night before that were not breakfast appropriate.

"Is something wrong?" she asked.

If he didn't want to embarrass himself, yes.

"No," he said and reached for a windbreaker in the closet. "I was just considering a jacket." He folded it over his arm and carried it in front of him as they headed downstairs to eat.

"Miss Drake?" a voice called out as they reached the lobby and headed toward the great hall.

They both stopped, turning their attention to the front desk where a clerk was looking their way. The woman had an envelope in her hand that looked eerily familiar.

Sebastian's empty stomach started to ache with the feeling of dread. It was a similar envelope to the one Harper had received on the plane. He wasn't sure why that surprised him. She hadn't met last night's blackmail request, so another note had arrived. He hadn't been in the lobby to see who had left it there. When he'd mentioned seeing Quentin loitering around the desk the night before, Harper hadn't seemed surprised, which had just reinforced his idea that he was the suspect to watch.

"I have a message here for you, ma'am," the clerk added in a thick Irish accent.

Harper knew what it was, too. They walked together to the front desk and she took the envelope from the woman's hand. It had her name written on it in the same nondescript block text. "Thank you," she said.

"Did you happen to be working when they left the note? To see who left it?" Sebastian asked.

"No, sir. I just started my shift. The previous clerk said it had been left at the desk early this morning while she was setting up the coffee station. She didn't see who left it, either. Is there a problem?"

"No," Sebastian said with a reassuring smile. "Thanks so much." He turned back to Harper, who was looking at the envelope with a face almost as white as the parchment. "Let's take that back upstairs," he suggested. "Breakfast can wait."

She nodded blankly and let him lead her out of the lobby. He glanced around, looking for someone loitering curiously in the area, but it was mostly empty. A couple he didn't recognize was looking at magazines in the corner, but there was no one else there. They were all likely in the great room gathering for their first authentic Irish breakfast.

Back in the room, he escorted Harper over to the love seat and sat beside her.

"You know, with everything else going on last night, I almost forgot I was missing the deadline. This morning, the thought hadn't even crossed my mind. How could I forget about something like that? And then I saw the envelope in her hand and I remembered what a mess I was still in. Now I don't want to open it," she said.

"Why not?"

"Because…it's not going to be good. He's going to be angry because I didn't pay the blackmail money. There's one of two things in this note—a second chance to pay or notification that my secret is as good as public knowledge by now. I could walk into the dining hall and everyone could know the truth about me."

"You won't know which it is until you open it."

With a sigh, she ran her finger under the lip of the envelope and ripped it open. She pulled out another small card, identical to the first, with the same block-style text inside. Harper held it up to read aloud.

"'It seems your payment got lost in the mail, Harper. Yesterday was a tiring day of travel, so I'm going to be kind and give you another opportunity to give me what I want. This time, to make it easier, make it one hundred thousand euros in an envelope at the front desk by noon tomorrow. Don't disappoint me again.'"

Harper's hand dropped into her lap with dismay. "Great, now the price has gone up. When I looked at the exchange rate yesterday, it was in the euro's favor. He's now asking for something in the neighborhood of a hundred and twenty thousand dollars in the name of 'convenience.' I mean, why not?" She giggled, bringing her hand to her mouth just in time to stifle a sob. "I couldn't pay the hundred grand, so two days later, naturally, I should be able to pay that and more."

Sebastian wrapped his arm around Harper's shoulders and pulled her tight against him. She gave in to the embrace, burying her face in his chest and holding on to him. He hated seeing her upset. He wasn't a very physical person by nature, but if he got his hands on her blackmailer, he wasn't sure what he would do. At the moment he wanted to choke the guy until tears ran down his cheeks like Harper's did.

"What am I going to do?" She sniffled against his polo shirt. "He's not going to go away. I don't have the money. I don't know what to do, Sebastian."

He sighed and stroked her hair as he tried to come up with an answer. He wasn't sure there was a way out of this that wouldn't be painful somehow. "Do you trust any of your friends enough? Lucy or Emma maybe? Your brother perhaps?"

"Trust them enough for what?"

"Enough to ask them to help you with this. To

give you the money. Just a loan until you get to your birthday and can pay them back."

Harper pulled away and shook her head. She wiped the tears from her cheeks, leaving black smudges of mascara that he wanted to reach out and brush away.

"I can't do that. I just can't."

"You don't think they'd give it to you?"

"No, they would. Each and every one of them would in a heartbeat," Harper explained. "That's why I can't ask. I'm not going to abuse their friendship like that. Besides, they'd want to know what it was for. They'd worry that I was in some kind of trouble."

"Aren't you?" he asked.

"Yes, but not trouble I want any of them to know about. This whole thing is so embarrassing. Really, even if I wasn't at risk of losing my inheritance, I wouldn't want anyone to know about the financial trouble I'm in. I'm an accountant. It just looks so awful."

Sebastian gently stroked her back, considering his options in this situation. Initially he hadn't been in favor of paying the blackmail, but this wasn't going to go away. This person was going to get the money or ruin Harper's life in the process. "What about the bank?" he asked.

She looked up at him, confusion creasing her brow. "What do you mean?"

"What about seeing if the local bank would lend

you the money? When we go into town today, we can stop at a bank and see what options you have."

"Not many," she said. "Without collateral, getting that much money would be nearly impossible. If by some chance they did agree to loan me the money, it would be at an outrageous interest rate."

"Not necessarily," Sebastian said thoughtfully. "What if I cosigned?"

Harper sat back against the arm of the love seat and looked at him with an expression he couldn't quite read. "Are you serious?"

He shrugged. "Yeah."

"That's really sweet of you to offer, Sebastian, but I can't ask you to do that. It wouldn't be right."

"Why? I have no intention of paying a dime of the money back. It's all on you. And if you don't pay it when your inheritance comes through, I'll see to it that there are unpleasant consequences for you, if it makes you feel better about it."

She blinked a few times as though she were trying to process his offer. "You'd really do that for me?"

"Of course," he said. "You're my girlfriend. Don't you think the blackmailer would think it suspicious if you couldn't come up with the money somehow and yet your boyfriend is a millionaire?"

Sebastian wasn't sure what the reaction would be, but he certainly wasn't expecting her to throw herself into his arms. Before he knew what was happening, Harper's lips were pressed to his once again. Just like at Neiman Marcus, she was enthusiastically thanking him with her mouth. Unlike at Neiman Marcus, this time there wasn't a crowd of onlookers to keep the kiss PG-rated.

If he was honest with himself, he'd been wanting this kiss since that one had ended. Not one of the quick pecks she gave him when they were out in public, but a real kiss. One where he could taste the cool mint-toothpaste flavor on her tongue and let his hands roam until they discovered that under today's long-sleeved T-shirt she was wearing a lace bra.

The kiss intensified as his palms cupped her through her shirt. Harper moaned softly against his mouth and moved closer to him on the love seat. It would be so easy to pull her into his lap, whip the shirt off her head and bury his face between the creamy breasts he'd only glimpsed the night before. But he wouldn't. Not now.

As much as he didn't want to, Sebastian forced himself to pull away. This wasn't the time or place for this to happen. If he and Harper ever transitioned from a fake relationship to a real one, he didn't want it to be because she was emotionally compromised or felt indebted to him.

He rested his forehead against hers as he took a cleansing breath and chuckled to himself.

"What's the laugh for?" she asked.

"I was just thinking that I would've offered to co-sign yesterday if I'd known I'd get that kiss in return."

Harper grimaced and shook her head with mock dismay. "Let's get back downstairs. We don't want to miss the bus to Sligo."

Six

"Wipe that anxious look off your face."

Harper clutched her purse to her chest and frowned at Sebastian. "I can't help it," she argued. "I don't like walking around with this much cash."

"You're not walking through downtown Manhattan. You're riding a bus with friends through the Irish countryside. We'll be back at the castle in a few minutes. No one on the bus is going to mug you, I'm pretty sure."

She could only sigh and shake her head, diverting her attention out the window to the passing scenery. Ireland was a beautiful country with rolling, emerald hillsides, misty valleys and wild, gray seas. She wished she was able to enjoy it. Harper had always wanted to go to Ireland but never managed to make the trip before. But now that she was here, all she could think about was the twenty-five thousand euros in her Birkin purse and the bastard she was about to give it to.

"Maybe B. Mayler is on the bus. Ever think of that? Maybe he followed us into town."

Sebastian turned to look over his shoulder at the people on the bus. "I doubt it. Besides, he wouldn't need to steal it from you. You're about to give it to him outright."

He was probably right. She hadn't seen Quentin on the bus or in town. She half expected to see him sitting in the lobby when they arrived, waiting with baited breath for her to leave the package at the front desk, especially after Sebastian had seen him at the desk the night before. She hated to tell Quentin that he was going to be disappointed.

Twenty-five thousand euros. Not a hundred thousand. That was all the bank would give her even with Sebastian's signature on the loan. If they'd had more time…if she'd had better credit, more collateral…if Harper'd had ties to Ireland… Their reasons for limiting the amount of the loan had gone on and on. She supposed she should be happy to have gotten this much. She was a quarter of the way there. Maybe it would keep the blackmailer happy until she could get more.

Looking into her purse for the twentieth time,

Harper checked to make sure the bundle of bills was still there. It was in a white envelope, labeled as directed, and included a note that explained this was all she could get until she returned to the United States. She intended to leave the package at the front desk as they went in. Then, maybe, she would be able to take a deep breath for the first time since she'd spied that envelope on her plane seat.

Or perhaps not.

As they pulled up the curved gravel driveway of Markree Castle, she closed her bag to make sure the envelope wouldn't fall out. Sebastian stayed close by her side as they exited the bus and walked into the hotel.

Despite their situation, it was nice to have him be there for her. He hadn't signed up for any of this drama when he'd agreed to come on the trip as her boyfriend. He'd been promised a free vacation and instead he'd been roped into a blackmail plot. And yet he hadn't complained. He'd been her sounding board, her shoulder to cry on and, at the moment, her personal bodyguard. Harper didn't know how to thank him for everything he'd done so far. If she'd come on this trip alone, she wasn't sure what she would've done.

They stopped at the desk long enough for her to hand over the package with instructions for the desk clerk. She slipped it into a blank mail slot on the back wall and went to answer the phone as though it was nothing to her. Harper supposed it was. Just something left for a guest. Who would imagine it was filled with thousands of euros in cash?

"Let's go upstairs," Sebastian suggested. "We need to get away from the desk so he can come pick it up."

Harper didn't argue. She just took his arm and let him lead her away. It felt good to cling to him, to have the strong support of his body against her own. It meant so much to have him there for her. It had been a long time since she'd had that in her life. When so much of her day-to-day existence was a lie, it was almost impossible to let people in. Even her best girlfriends, the people who knew her better than anyone, didn't know the whole truth about her.

As they stepped inside their room and he closed the door behind them, she realized how lonely she had been. Even when she had been with Quentin, something had been missing. She was holding part of herself back from everyone, never letting anyone completely in.

But Sebastian knew all her secrets. And he was still there with her. At least for now.

Harper didn't expect him to stay around after the end of the trip. He had a life to return to and so did she. But they had the here and now together and, for her, that was enough. She just needed to feel like she wasn't going through this by herself. She wasn't lonely when he was around. She didn't have to pretend to be someone she wasn't. It was such a relief to be able to let her guard down and just relax into who she really was for the first time in forever.

She turned to look at Sebastian. His large, dark eyes were watching her from across the room the way they always did. He constantly seemed to be in silent study of the world around him. Of her. Perhaps it was the engineer in him, taking things apart and putting them back together in his mind. Figuring out how things worked. What made them tick. What made her tick. The idea of him instinctively knowing just how to push her buttons was enough to make her need to slip out of her suddenly too warm jacket.

He was one of the most intense men she'd ever encountered. And now, in this moment, she wanted to lose herself in that intensity.

"Sebastian."

It was all she said, yet she knew her tone conveyed so much more to him than just his name. He bit thoughtfully at his full bottom lip as his gaze narrowed at her. At last, he started moving toward her at an unhurried pace. Their gazes never broke away from one another as he came nearer. And even when he was close enough to reach out and pull Harper into his arms, he didn't touch her. He just studied her, taking in every inch from her dark ponytail to the cobblestone-scuffed deck shoes she'd worn into town.

This was her move to make. Their relationship was set up with parameters she'd defined. If they were going to cross a line, she had to be the one to do it. And that was fine by her.

Her lips met his before she could lose her nerve. Their kiss this morning had been proof that there was more between them than just some arrangement. Excitement and gratitude had overridden her good sense then, but the kiss had been about anything but saying thank you. The current running beneath the surface was one of mutual attraction, undeniable chemistry… they had just been holding back out of respect for the agreement they'd made. This relationship was supposed to be all for show, right?

But all that went out the window when he looked at her the way he did. Touched her the way he did.

"Make me forget about all of this," she said in a desperate whisper against the rough stubble of his cheek.

Sebastian didn't hesitate to give her what she'd asked for. Within seconds her shirt was over her head. His hungry mouth traveled down her chin and throat to bury in the valley between her breasts. He nipped at her delicate skin with his teeth even as he unclasped her bra and cast it to the floor.

The sensations were so overwhelming, all Harper could do was close her eyes and try to take it all in. His hands moved quickly to cover her exposed breasts. She groaned as her tight, sensitive nipples grazed his rough palms. His fingertips pressed into her flesh, squeezing and kneading her breasts.

The moment he drew one tight bud into his mouth, Harper's head fell back and she cried out to the ceiling. His silky, hot tongue bathed her skin, sucking hard and then biting gently with his teeth until she gasped. She gripped his head, trying to pull him closer as she buried her fingers in the dark waves of his hair. She couldn't get close enough.

Then he pulled away.

Sebastian stood fully upright for a moment, his hands encircling her waist. He held her steady there as his dark eyes studied her face. He seemed to take in every detail, from the curve of her lips to the scar across her brow where she'd fallen out of a bunk bed as a child.

Harper suddenly felt self-conscious as she stood there, topless and exposed to his scrutiny. What would he see if he looked that closely? She wanted to turn off the lights, to cover up, pull away before he found something he didn't like about her body.

Then he shook his head and said, "Beautiful," under his breath and she tried to put those worries aside to be the beautiful woman on the inside that he saw on the outside.

With his firm grip on her, he pulled her across the wooden floor to their four-poster bed. He pushed her back until she was sitting on the edge. Harper eased back just as he moved forward, planting his left knee and fist into the soft mattress beside her. Hovering over her, he used his right hand to trace faint circles across her stomach.

It both tickled and turned her on at the same time. She tried hard not to squirm under his touch, but her body couldn't stay still. She ached to move closer and pull away all at once. Then he moved down and brushed his fingers over the button of her jeans. With a quick snap, they were undone and he pulled the zipper down to the base. He probed under the fabric, tracing over the lace that protected her center.

Harper gasped as he grazed her most sensitive spot once, twice, then a third time, more forcefully, making her back arch up off the bed.

Sebastian's gaze fixed on her. Ever the engineer, he studied her expressions and her every reaction to his touch. With a satisfied smirk, he eased back and hooked his fingers beneath her jeans. He slid them over her hips and down her legs, throwing them to the floor.

His hands replaced the denim, sliding back up her legs and gliding over every inch of her skin. His mouth followed in their wake, leaving searing kisses along the insides of her ankles, calves, knees and inner thighs. When he reached her panties, Harper expected him to pull them off like he had with her jeans. Instead he grasped the side with his fist and tugged hard until the pieces came off in his hand. He threw the torn strips of fabric away.

"That's much better." With nothing else in his way,

he pressed her thighs further apart and leaned in to lap his tongue over the newly exposed flesh.

The sensation was like a lightning bolt through her core.

"You're buying me new panties," she gasped. "Those were twenty-five dollars and I can't afford to replace them."

"Fine," Sebastian said. "I'll buy. You three pairs. For every one. I destroy." With each pause in his speech, his tongue flicked over her again.

"Are you planning to rip them all?"

"It depends." He spread her legs wider and moved his mouth more furiously over Harper until she was once again squirming beneath him.

"Depends on what?" Harper gasped and gripped the blankets beneath her in tight fists.

"On whether or not they get in my way."

Harper made a mental note to keep her nicer panties in her luggage. That was her last coherent thought.

At that moment Sebastian slid two fingers inside her. He thrust them deep, positioning the heel of his hand to grind against her clit. His whole hand started moving and she began to unravel. The combination was like nothing she'd ever felt before. She found herself yelling out, gasping and crying, even long before her release. The sensations were almost overpowering.

Her orgasm came fast and furiously. She wasn't prepared for how hard the pulsating waves would pound her body. She shuddered and rocked against his hand, shouting with the power of her release until it had nearly zapped all her strength. It took all she had to reach down and grab his hand, pulling it away from her. She couldn't take any more. Not quite yet, at least.

Harper closed her eyes and collapsed against the mattress. Her skin was pink and flushed, the butterflies still fluttering inside her. She swallowed hard, noting her raw throat as she gasped for breath. She wasn't entirely sure what she'd expected from Sebastian, but it hadn't been that. She'd never experienced an orgasm like that in her life. It was intense. Overwhelming. Amazing. And as soon as she recovered, she wanted to do it again.

Sebastian's weight shifted on the bed and she heard him walk into the bathroom. She opened her eyes when she heard him come back in. He had gotten rid of his clothes and replaced them with his pajama pants.

Bending down, he scooped her into his arms and placed her properly onto the bed. He crawled in beside her and tugged the blankets over them both.

Harper was surprised. She didn't think they were finished. She was great, of course, but she thought for sure that he would want some for himself. Maybe he didn't have protection with him. She'd have to be sure to correct that before they got together again.

Instead, he rolled onto his side and wrapped his

arms around her, pulling her into the warm nook of his body. It was unexpected, but perhaps exactly what she needed.

"What are you thinking about?" he asked.

"Not a damn thing," Harper said. She could barely string together a coherent sentence at this point.

"Good. Mission accomplished," he said.

"You know what I've noticed?"

Sebastian clung to consciousness long enough to make a thoughtful sound in response to Harper's question. "Mmm?"

"I've realized that I really don't know anything about you, but you know everything about me."

The question was enough to jerk him from the comfortable nap he'd almost settled into. Apparently the post-coital bliss he'd induced in her was short-lived and her mind was spinning again. With his eyes wide open now, he sighed. "That's not true. We met up before the trip and talked about each other for the cover story."

Harper snuggled against his chest and let her fingers twirl through his dark chest hair. "Yes. We talked about a few things, but you were pretty light on details. You know all my deepest, darkest secrets and all I know is that you went to MIT."

"There's not much more about me to tell," he said. It was a lie, but the one he preferred people to believe. "I had a very boring, uneventful life before I went to college and met Finn. Then we started a business, invented some stuff and got rich in the process. My life is still boring, I just have more money. Unlike you, there's no secret dramas, no trust fund stipulations, no blackmail plots. You're not missing out on much with me, I promise."

Now it was Harper's turn to make a thoughtful sound. Eventually she stilled and her breathing became soft and even against his chest. Of course, she had riled him up and fallen asleep, leaving him lying in bed with a brain no longer interested in sleep.

Part of him felt bad about lying to Harper mere minutes after giving her an orgasm. She had been brutally honest with him about her life, but that was out of necessity, not out of a willingness to share her past with him. He'd been sucked into her blackmail plot or he was certain she wouldn't have told him, just like she hadn't told anyone else. He was just there. And he was okay with that. She just shouldn't expect him to reciprocate.

It wasn't because he had huge skeletons in his own closet. His uncle Joe had gotten a DUI for driving his riding lawnmower to the gas station drunk to get more beer. That was the closest his family had come to brushes with the law. No scandals. No secrets. They were just the one thing that he couldn't be once he'd found himself dropped into the world of Manhattan society against his will—poor.

Harper had been angry with him initially for not

telling her that he was rich. It was her presumption that he wasn't—he hadn't said anything either way. He typically didn't. Sebastian wasn't the kind to present himself like the usual power-hungry Manhattan CEO, so most people wouldn't think he was, much less believe him if he insisted otherwise. Finn was the suave one: well-dressed, well-spoken, well-traveled. He reeked of money and prestige. No one ever questioned that he was the president of BioTech.

Sebastian flew under the radar and he liked it that way. He didn't like the way people changed around him when they found out he was rich. All of a sudden people acted like he was more important and things he said were more interesting. He'd go from being mostly ignored to receiving invitations to play racquetball at the club. He didn't play racquetball and had no intention of starting. It was all perception. His wealth shaped how people saw him.

And the same would be true if his rich friends found out he'd come from a dirt-poor background.

At the moment he was sleeping under the same roof as some of the most powerful business owners and billionaires in Manhattan. When he'd been introduced as one of them, they'd welcomed him with open arms. He was good enough for Harper, he owned his own company…he must be good people. But would they respond differently if they knew he was fifteen years removed from what they considered to be poor white trash? That his parents would be living in the same trailer he'd grown up in if he hadn't bought them a house with his first million?

Harper had money troubles of her own, but even at her poorest, she had more money than his family'd had growing up. He'd had to bust his ass to earn scholarships and get through college to build a career and wealth of his own. None of it had been given to him by his daddy or grandpa or anyone else.

While he'd been sympathetic to her plight when she'd told him about blowing her first two-million inheritance, a part of him had winced internally at the thought of it. Finn had some family money that helped them get started, but it was nowhere near enough. What could Sebastian have done if someone had handed him two million to get BioTech off the ground? They could've gotten a decent facility up and running instead of working out of a garage the first year. They could've gotten their first major product into production years earlier.

And she'd blown it on purses and shoes.

Harper had obviously grown up a lot in the years since she'd made those mistakes. She'd not only managed to support herself, but do a good enough job at it that no one questioned that she wasn't still rich. But with that big balloon payment looming in her future, he had to wonder if she would be back to her old habits.

It would take longer to blow through twenty-eight million, but she could still do it. Then what? There would be no third payment to bail her out again unless some rich relative died.

Or she married well. To a rich CEO perhaps?

Sebastian sighed and looked down at Harper as she slept peacefully on his chest. He didn't want to think that way about her. She hadn't seemed at all like the typical Manhattan gold digger. But she certainly had seemed a lot more interested in him once she'd realized he was rich and not just some wheelchair salesman. Yes, he could easily revive the glamorous lifestyle she had once lived. Since things between them had accelerated so quickly, a part of him worried about her motivations.

She'd been completely in love with that creep Quentin only two years ago. A guy who might very well be blackmailing her right now. She herself had said she didn't have the greatest taste in men, and choosing Quentin certainly seemed like a style over substance choice in his opinion.

That said, she genuinely seemed attracted to Sebastian. She hadn't asked anything of him, even though they both knew he could pay off that blackmail and put an end to it all. If it would ever end. She'd barely agreed to let him cosign the loan. And yet part of him was still concerned about what Harper was after.

He didn't mind getting physically closer to her. He was happy to. Holding her warm, soft body in his arms was one of the best things to happen to him in a long time. He actually wished he could've taken this afternoon further, but he knew putting the brakes on when he had was the right choice for now. He'd felt his heart racing uncomfortably in his chest as she'd come and had decided he needed to stop there. He'd promised to help her forget her problems and he'd done that.

The doctor had told him he would know if he was feeling well enough to indulge. It had been almost a week since his attack, so hopefully that would be soon. But that was about as far as he was willing to go with Harper. At least for now. There were too many unknowns, too many balls in the air for him to let this fake relationship develop past much more than a simple vacation fling.

Once they were back in New York, he would return to his lab, she would inherit her fortune and they'd likely go their separate ways. He didn't have time for a relationship and she wouldn't need his help any longer. Things would fall apart. So planning for the worst, Sebastian intended to keep his distance.

Seven

This was too easy, really.

Although she was hardly a criminal master-mind—she'd never committed a crime in her life before this trip—this wasn't proving that difficult. All she'd had to do was tell the woman at the desk that she needed a new room key. The overly trusting employee had made a new one for her without question or identification and handed it over. After all, they were all friends and family here for a wedding. Certainly a trustworthy crowd...

Then all she had to do was wait. Today's itinerary included a trip to a few tourist destinations of interest, including a local abbey and a ruin of another old castle. She'd feigned a migraine and stayed at the hotel while everyone else loaded into the buses to go.

Once she was certain they were good and truly gone, she made her way to Harper's room. The door opened right up, revealing the relatively tidy space. She took her time looking around at the antique furniture and heavy velvet drapes. The room was much nicer than the one she was staying in, but she wasn't one of the bride's best friends like Harper was.

After the courier she'd hired picked up the package at the front desk and brought it to her in the castle's east gardens, she'd been certain her plan was a success. Then she saw the note inside and counted only a quarter of what she'd been expecting. It was a lot of money to be sure, but not enough.

Harper seemed to think that she was the one in control of this situation. That she could just not pay, for whatever reasons she could come up with, and everything would be okay. That was not the case. That meant taking her threat up a notch.

She'd only intended to leave a note in the room. She'd wanted to invade Harper's space and unnerve her by showing what she could do if she wanted to. But once she was there, she realized she had an opportunity to make this a more lucrative visit and create a huge impact at the same time. She opened the largest piece of luggage and dug around inside. Most of the clothes were hanging in the closet, so all that was left in the bag were some intimates and a Louis Vuitton jewelry roll tied up with a leather cord. Bingo.

She unrolled the bundle, looking over the neatly organized pieces of jewelry in the different pockets. A few looked like nice costume jewelry, but in one pouch she pulled out a pair of diamond stud earrings that were at least one carat each. She slipped them into her purse, following with a necklace with a fat, pear-shaped sapphire pendant. Last, she pocketed a diamond-and-ruby tennis bracelet and an aquamarine-and-diamond cocktail ring. All nice, but somehow she'd expected more from Harper. Maybe she'd left her pricier pieces at home this trip.

In the other piece of luggage, Sebastian's she assumed, she found a fancy pair of gold-and-emerald cufflinks in a velvet box and an old pocket watch. She wasn't a jeweler, but she knew enough to estimate that she'd made up for a good chunk of the money Harper had shorted her. It was a start, at least. She'd have a jeweler back in the States appraise her haul later.

Harper seemed to think there was no way she could come up with the money, but she just wasn't putting her mind to it. Just flipping through the clothes in the closet, she spied a couple designer pieces that would fetch a pretty penny on Poshmark. The Hermès Birkin purse she was carrying the other day would, too. There was a waiting list to get one of those bags. Even the case she kept her jewelry in was worth at least a couple hundred dollars.

Harper had a lot of expensive things. There wasn't a single designer piece in her own closet, but then again, she wasn't pretending to be rich. Having these things was all part of Harper's ruse. Of course, if she could get her hands on stuff this nice just to fake out her friends and family, she could get the money, too.

Part of her wanted to blow the top off Harper's whole lie just to expose how shallow she was. What a horrible thing it was to be poor! She was just trying to make it by until that next big payment from grand-dad, then everything would be okay again. In their lifetimes, most people would never see the amount of money she'd already blown, never mind what she was set to inherit later.

There were worse things than being poor in this world. Perhaps being shallow? Being a liar? Maybe even a thief? She laughed at that thought. She didn't look at this as theft. She was just an instrument of karma in this scenario. If she got a tiny piece of the pie in the process, that was just a bonus.

She turned around and looked at the tidy, elegant room. Housekeeping had already come for the morning and left chocolates on the pillows. It hadn't been a part of her original plan, but she decided on the spot that it could use a little redecorating. Just to make the place look lived in, of course.

When she was out of breath and the room looked

like it had been hit by a tornado, she took the white envelope out of her pocket and left it on the nightstand.

She had officially turned up the heat on Miss Drake.

They'd spent a long afternoon touring the Irish countryside and Sebastian had enjoyed it. It was a quiet, peaceful country to just sit and soak in the atmosphere. A good choice for a vacation location and he was sure his doctor would approve. Outside Dublin, most of the towns were small and laid back. No honking taxis and aggressive panhandlers. Just old historic sites and friendly people, all with stories to tell.

Despite the peaceful scenery, having Harper in the seat beside him on the bus had the opposite effect. The nearness of her kept his pulse fairly high. Every now and then he would get a whiff of her perfume. She would lean in to him to say something, touch his knee and playfully kiss him. At this point, the lines of their relationship were so blurry, he didn't know if she was really kissing *him* or if it was all for show. Though if people were suspicious of their relationship, it was a little too late to care. The wedding was tomorrow. They would be back in the US before long.

So did she mean it?

Sebastian tried not to overthink it. Instead he turned back to his notebook and worked on a sketch he'd started at the abbey. It seemed an odd place to get inspiration for medical equipment, but there had been a statue in the museum that was wearing some kind of armor. The shape of how it fit to the knight's leg had got him to thinking about prosthetic and robotic legs in a whole new way. That was all it had taken for him to lose all interest in old churches and to turn his focus back to work.

"You're not even listening," he heard Harper say.

Snapping out of the zone, Sebastian looked up. "What?"

"You're a million miles away. Did you hear a word I said?"

He shook his head sheepishly. "I didn't. I was focused on my work."

"I thought so. What is that?"

He sighed and looked at the rough sketch. It would take a lot of refinement for the doodle to become a cutting-edge piece of equipment, but it was a start. "One day, it may be BioTech's latest design for a robotic prosthetic. This one is for the leg."

She looked at the sketch thoughtfully. "Is that the kind of thing you usually work on?"

He shrugged. "It varies. Our very first product, the one that put us up with the big boys, was a prosthetic arm. Looking back at it now, it seems like such a crude design, but it changed everything for patients at the time. Lately we've been using 3D printing to develop custom fits for patients. Insurance wouldn't pay for something like that, so most people couldn't afford a customized fit until now. That's made a huge difference in comfort for people who've lost limbs."

"Do you work a lot with soldiers?"

"Yes. We also work with accident victims or people born with various birth defects. That's only part of what we do there. My latest project is for paraplegics. If I can get a successful prototype finished—one that can be produced affordably enough—it could change the lives of thousands of people that are wheelchair bound. This sketch is part of that."

There was a long silence and when Sebastian turned to look at Harper, he realized she was staring at him, not his sketches. "What?" he asked.

She smiled and reached out to brush a chunk of dark hair from his eyes. "I've never seen you like this."

"Like how?" He looked down to take inventory of himself self-consciously.

"I've never experienced your passion for your work. I guess I thought you were just another guy making a buck on medical research, but you really seem to care about what you're doing. Your work is amazing."

"Thank you," he responded awkwardly.

It always made him uncomfortable when people gushed at him about his research. He didn't do it for the feel-good factor. He did it for people like his brother who faced a lifetime lived with physical limitations. If he could finish the exo-legs, it meant he would have accomplished his biggest dream. Seeing his older brother walk again would mean he'd finally succeeded. The money, the success, the praise…it was all nice, but that wasn't what he wanted. He wanted to see the look on his mother's face when she saw her oldest son walk across the room unassisted. To him, that was worth sacrificing most of his life. Unfortunately he'd pushed too far and almost sacrificed all of it.

"So what inspired you to go into this line of work?" she asked.

He'd been waiting for that question. That was a slippery slope in conversation and Sebastian wasn't ready to go there. Not with reporters and not with Harper. He had a prepared answer for those times, however. He'd done several interviews and never wanted to bring his brother or his past into the discussion. It wasn't because he was embarrassed to talk about his brother's accident or his family situation. It was more that he wanted to maintain their privacy as well as his own. He didn't need the headline claiming he was a "rags to riches" success driven by his poor brother's tragic accident. That simplified the story far too much.

"I was always interested in robotics and engineering," he began his practiced story. "When I met up with Finn, he was in medical school and we got the idea to combine our specialties and start a company together after graduation. It was easy to develop a passion for the work when you see how it can impact people's lives."

"I imagine it is. I'm a corporate accountant for Jonah's company. There's no passion there, but I'm good with numbers so I got a finance degree. We're a video game company, though. It's hardly important work."

"It's important work to the people that love to play those games. Every job is critical in a different way. Finn says I'm a workaholic, but when you're doing something that can change someone's life, how do you justify walking away from your desk for a moment? Especially for something as trivial as a vacation?"

"I guess it's about balance. You don't want to burn out. But look—here you are on a vacation. Sounds like that's a big step for you."

Sebastian chuckled to himself. She had no idea. "It is. I haven't been out of my labs this long since we started the company ten years ago."

"So how were you able to do it now?"

He tensed in his seat. What was he going to say? A doctor-enforced break? Not the answer he wanted to give. He was supposed to be a successful guy. He didn't want to show weakness to Harper or any of the other people on this trip. Like a pack of wild animals, they could easily turn on the weakest member. He didn't want to give any of them the ammunition to come for him. Not his background, not his health, not his fake/real relationship with Harper. If he let out too much about himself, he might be the next one blackmailed.

"You gave me no choice," he said with a laugh. "A beautiful woman walks up to me in a department store, asks me out and offers me a free trip to Ireland. How can any red-blooded man pass that up?"

Looking up, Sebastian noticed they had reached the hotel. He was relieved to end the conversation there. "Looks like we're back."

Everyone gathered their things and shuffled back into the hotel. The arrival couldn't have been better timed. He was more than happy to stop talking about himself. All he wanted to do now was to go upstairs, take a hot shower and get ready for dinner. Tonight they were hosting some kind of authentic Irish dinner show at the castle with traditional music and dance. It sounded interesting enough.

"I'm ready to take off these shoes," Harper said as she slipped her key card into the door. She took two steps and stopped short, sending him slamming into her back.

"What's wrong?"

Harper pushed open the door and revealed the mess that had once been their hotel room. Their things were scattered everywhere. Furniture was overturned. It was awful.

"Don't touch anything," he said. "We've been robbed."

"Don't touch anything?" Harper asked. "What are we going to do? Call the police?"

"That was my thought."

Harper walked into the room and picked up a familiar white envelope sitting on the nightstand. "Think again. If we call the cops, the blackmailer will expose me for sure."

With a sigh, Sebastian slammed the door shut and walked in to survey the mess. "So what does it say? I take it he wasn't pleased by the partial payment."

"It says that he's taken a few things to make up for the missing money. That was just a punishment, though. He still expects a hundred and twenty thousand dollars before the wedding reception ends." She looked up with despair in her eyes. "What about the twenty-five thousand euros he's already got? It's like it didn't even count. That or he's just jacking up the fee every time we miss a deadline." She dropped her face into her hands. "This is never going to end."

Sebastian walked over and sat beside her on the mattress. "It will end. He can't string this along forever. You're going to turn thirty and once you inherit, there's nothing to hold over your head. Or he exposes you and there's no money to be had. But it will end." He wrapped his arm around her shoulders. It wasn't the best pep talk he'd ever given, but it was something.

He didn't know what else to say as they sat and looked at their destroyed hotel suite. It must have taken quite a bit of time to do it, but given they'd been gone for hours, the blackmailer had had all the time in the world.

"Did you bring anything valuable?" he asked.

"Just a few things. Mainly pieces I was going to wear to the wedding." Harper got up and sought out her overturned suitcase. "My jewelry roll is gone. Oh, wait…" She spied it in the corner and picked it up. She poked through a couple pockets and shook her head. "He got all the good stuff. That sapphire neck-lace belonged to my mother," she said, tears shim-mering in her eyes.

Sebastian cursed and stood to go to her. "We can call the cops. We don't have to mention the blackmail. You'll need the report for your insurance claims."

"What insurance?" she chuckled sadly. "You're talking like I have the money to insure all this stuff. I don't. It's gone. It's all just gone. Probably forty thousand dollars' worth of jewelry, easy. Did you bring anything?"

Sebastian hadn't really thought about his things. He hadn't previously been a target of the blackmailer, but he supposed if they wanted money, they'd get it from anywhere. "Not much," he said. Looking around, he found the box with his cufflinks for his tuxedo. It was empty. Figures. The only other item he had with him was his grandfather's pocket watch, but it wasn't worth anything. He carried it for sen-timental value.

He dug around in his stuff, flinging pillows out of the way, but found that it, too, was gone. He turned a chair right-side up and sat with a disgusted huff.

"What did he get?" Harper looked at him with wide eyes of concern.

"My great-grandfather's pocket watch," he said. "He was a train conductor. It's not worth a dime to anyone but me. I can't believe the bastard took it."

Harper groaned. "Oh, no. I'll replace anything you lost once I get my money," she offered. "I know I can't replace your grandfather's watch exactly, but I'll do whatever I can. I'm so sorry to have dragged you into this whole mess."

"It's not your fault," Sebastian said. "But we've got to find a way to put an end to it all. Maybe I just need to give you the money."

"Sebastian, no," she said, crouching at his knee. She looked up at him with a dismayed expression. "I can't ask you to do that. You've already done too much."

He shook his head. "I don't want to pay him. He doesn't deserve the damn money, but it might be the only answer we have. But if we do pay him," he said with angrily gritted teeth, "I want all our stuff back."

"So what do we know about this Josie?" Lucy asked in a hushed voice over a delicate china plate of tea sandwiches.

They were at Violet's bridal tea, a ladies-only

event. All the men, Sebastian included, had gone to play a round of golf, followed by some day drinking that would likely run until the rehearsal dinner. This was one of Harper's first real opportunities to sit with her friends without Sebastian or the other guys since they'd arrived in Ireland.

Violet was at another table near the front, being adored by all the ladies in attendance, leaving Harper, Lucy and Emma to sit in the back corner and gossip as they often did. They all shrugged in response to Lucy's question, Harper included. She didn't know, or really care much about Quentin's new fiancée. She had bigger, more pressing worries, but she was interested in why the others were so concerned.

"I hadn't met her before the trip, but I had heard about her through the grapevine. To hear it told," Emma said as she gripped her teacup, "the engagement was quite the surprise to everyone. Given his current situation, I think a lot of people felt that Quentin might have chosen a woman with a fatter bank account and better connections. As far as I know, Josie is a broke nobody. She's a secretary for a financial firm or something. Not exactly what I was expecting. Of course, all that could've happened after he proposed and then he was stuck with her."

Harper perked up in her seat at Emma's story. "Given his current situation? Stuck? What do you mean by 'all that'?"

Emma and Lucy shared knowing glances before

turning back to Harper. "We hadn't said anything because bringing up Quentin in conversations always
seemed to put you in a bad mood."

"Yes, well, talking about someone's ex is hardly
a way to perk up their day. Unless it's bad news. Is
it bad news?"

Lucy nodded. Her dark eyes lit with excitement.
"Apparently he was cut off by his dear old dad."

Harper sat back in her seat, her jaw agape. That
certainly was news. Quentin was an attorney, but he
was a long way from being the successful hot shot
he pretended to be. Most of his money had come
from his family. When they were dating, she recalled
him getting a ten-thousand-dollar-a-week allowance
from his father. He'd been twenty-eight at the time,
giving Harper a run for her money when it came to
being spoiled.

"He's the low man on the totem pole at his law
firm," Harper said. "Without his allowance, he would
be in big trouble. He couldn't afford his apartment,
his car…he certainly couldn't afford the giant engagement ring I've seen her sporting, either."

"Exactly," Emma said.

"Do we know why he got cut off?" Harper asked.

Lucy shook her head. "I haven't heard anything
specific, but you know he had to have done something his dad really wasn't happy about to get cut off."

"So why would someone in his position propose to
a woman that won't be any help with that situation?

There are plenty of rich, single women in Manhattan that he could've chosen instead. He could've even come crawling back to you," Emma said.

"Not likely," Harper said. Quentin knew Harper didn't have any money or he might've tried. She couldn't tell the others that, though.

"What's so special about her?"

"I don't know. He loves her, maybe?" Harper replied with a sarcastic tone.

"Love? Quentin? Come on, now." Emma snorted. "If he was capable of that, he would've married you years ago. Maybe she's from an important family or one of his clients' children. No, my bet is that his father disapproves of the engagement and cut him off when he found out Quentin proposed. Unless she's got more to offer than meets the eye, I think he's searching for his relationship escape hatch. Once this wedding is over, he's going to drop her like a rock to get back in daddy's good graces. You just watch."

"Why would he propose to a woman his father didn't like?" Lucy asked. "Could she be pregnant?"

The three turned to where Josie was seated sipping tea. Her dress was fairly tight, showing no signs of a baby belly. "I doubt it," Harper said.

"I wonder if he just wanted to be engaged to someone at the wedding to make Harper jealous and it ended up backfiring on him."

Harper turned to Emma and frowned. "That's silly. Who would make up a fake relationship just to make someone else jealous?" The irony of the words were not lost on her.

"Maybe not jealous. Maybe he just didn't want to come here and face you on his own."

"He hasn't even spoken to me the whole trip. I doubt he's given me much thought at all."

"Well, you may be right, but I think it gives him the perfect motive to pick a random girl to be his fiancée for a few weeks."

Harper lifted her teacup and sipped thoughtfully. Being cut off by daddy also gave her the one piece of the puzzle she'd been missing—the perfect motive for Quentin to blackmail her.

Eight

Sebastian was exhausted from a day golfing with the others but keen to get back to Harper to tell her everything he'd overheard during the trip. Between eighteen holes and half a dozen beers, mouths had loosened among the gentlemen. In addition to getting to know them all better, he'd picked up some stock tips, improved his swing and gotten some more dirt on her ex, Quentin.

As the bus pulled up in front of the castle, he spied Harper walking out toward the east gardens. When they unloaded, he trotted off after her, catching up just as she reached the intricate hedges that outlined the borders. She sat on a stone bench that overlooked the formal pattern of flowerbeds in bright summer colors that contrasted with the lush green of the grass.

"Harper!"

She turned and looked over her shoulder at him. She was wearing a pretty, pale pink, eyelet sundress with a matching sweater. "Hey there, Arnold Palmer. How did the golf go?"

He strolled the rest of the way toward her to catch his breath. He needed to do more running, apparently. "Awful," he said as he dropped down beside her on the bench. "I couldn't tell them I'd never played before, so I had to fake it and claim I was rusty from working too much."

"You've never played golf? What kind of CEO are you?"

Sebastian chuckled. "The kind that doesn't take clients out to schmooze on the greens. That's Finn's job. I work. But I have played golf. Just not this kind. I'm used to the windmills and the alligators that swallow your ball if you putt it into the wrong hole."

"Miniature golf. You've played Putt-Putt. Yeah, I'd say that's a little different."

"I'll tell you, though. Once I got the ball near the hole, I was an excellent putter. Just took me five swings over par to get that close."

Harper winced and laughed. "Wow. Lose any money?"

He shook his head. "I'm not that stupid. There was no way I was betting on my game. I did offer Quentin a wager, though. I bet him a thousand dollars that he'd shank his next ball into a sand trap."

She arched her brow curiously. "And?"

Sebastian reached into his pocket and pulled out a roll of hundred dollar bills. "I think I jinxed him. He basically shot it straight into the sand dunes and couldn't get out. Completely rattled the guy. I didn't feel guilty about it, though. If he's your blackmailer, then this thousand may have come from the money you paid him yesterday. If that's true, then I'm glad to steal some back." He handed the cash over to Harper.

"What is this for?" she asked, looking at the bills uncurling in the palm of her hand.

"For whatever." He shrugged. "It's not my money, so you can light cigars with it for all I care. Pay it to the blackmailer. Pay it on the loan. Get a really expensive manicure. Save it for a rainy day. Whatever you want. Just spend it knowing that I took it from Quentin. That should make it all the sweeter."

Harper closed her fist around the money and nodded. "It will," she said before slipping it into the little wallet pocket of her cell phone case. "Anything else interesting come up this afternoon?"

"Lots of man talk. Mostly bluster without substance. It got a little heated about the Yankees once alcohol got involved. The groom's face turned as red as his hair when someone said something about the Mets being a better team. I was smart enough to stay out of that. I don't know enough about sports to comment intelligently."

"Really? You didn't play sports in school?"

Sebastian frowned. "No. That wasn't my thing," he said. He supposed it might've interested him if he'd had the time. Maybe the swim team. But the fees to participate in school sports had been too high and all his free time had been taken up by working to help support his family. He hadn't had the typical frivolous youth, but Harper didn't know that. "I did learn something interesting about Quentin, though."

Harper turned toward him on the stone bench. "Me, too. But you go first."

"Okay. While we were talking, someone mentioned that Quentin was in some legal hot water. Apparently he'd tried to flip some real estate and used shoddy contractors to save money. The people that bought the place took him to court and the judge sided with them, awarding them a settlement to correct some of the repairs. Guess for how much?"

"A hundred thousand dollars?"

"Bingo."

"That is interesting. It certainly gives him a reason to come after me for exactly that much money. Especially after what I learned about him at the tea party."

"What's that?"

"His father cut him off, financially. We're not sure if it's because he disapproves of the fiancée, or maybe because of his legal troubles, but he isn't getting any more money from his father. I can tell you that's huge. He's probably hurting for cash right now. Even that thousand-dollar loss to you today likely stings."

Sebastian only shrugged. "He should've turned down the bet, then. He's too cocky to think he will lose."

"That is Quentin for you. Looking back, I know I dodged a bullet with that one."

"I'm sure you did. For all your dating angst, I hear you're quite the catch. All the gentlemen I spoke to think rather highly of you," Sebastian added with a smile.

Harper blushed with embarrassment and pushed a stray strand of dark hair behind her ear in an endearing way. He liked the way she was wearing it today. It was down in loose waves, almost like wild morning-after hair. It made him think about how it had cascaded across the pillows the other afternoon as he'd pleasured her. When he'd touched it, it had felt like silk between his fingertips. He wanted to touch it again.

"Do they now?" Harper said. "What did they say?"

"Well, they all congratulated me for winning you over. They said you were an amazing woman and that I would be a fool to let you slip through my fingertips."

Sebastian knew their words to be true before the

men had confirmed it. Harper, however, seemed dumbfounded by the whole conversation.

"Really?"

"Yes, really."

"Even Quentin?"

Sebastian nodded. "Even Quentin. I don't know if it's all part of his game or not, but he said there were times when he knew he'd made the wrong choice letting you go."

Harper gasped. "I can't believe it."

"I don't know why. You're smart, beautiful, funny, sweet…"

"Quit buttering me up."

"You tend to lie a lot, though," he added with a smile. "Of course, they don't know that. They did mention that you have expensive tastes and might be costly to keep, but that you were worth it."

Harper laughed aloud at the final observation. "That sounds more like I was expecting to hear. How funny. Who knew golf with the boys could be so enlightening?"

It certainly had been for him. He'd already been dreading the end of the trip and their run as a couple, but his chat with the other men had made him wonder if maybe he shouldn't push harder for something more with Harper. Something beyond the physical. He'd been worried about letting himself get too close, but perhaps in time it might be possible. If he let himself do it. If he could take a step back from his work and allow life to take its place. Balance had never been his strength. He was balls-to-the-wall, all or nothing. Here, a relationship was easy because work wasn't interfering. Back home, the relationship would interfere with his work.

And that was only if Harper was open to the possibility. Now that he'd filled her head with compliments about how great a catch she was, he might not be what she wanted. He was a great stand-in for a boyfriend in a pinch, but would she want him once they were back in the States again? Maybe only if her grandfather cut her off.

"I guess the men's golf game is just as big a gossip cesspool as the ladies' tea," Harper said with a smile. "Did my brother say anything embarrassing?"

"Not much. He'd already said his peace to me a few days ago. The first day we arrived, actually."

Harper's eyes got big as she stiffened on the bench. She put her hand on him, squeezing his forearm. "What? No. What did he say?"

Sebastian chuckled. "Nothing too embarrassing, just basic big-brother stuff. I think he was just worried about you. He wanted to make sure my intentions were honest. He gave me a little insight into you, too."

"Like what?"

"Like, I'm not telling you," Sebastian retorted.

"So unfair. You've got all the insight into me and you're this puzzle box I can't get into." With a sigh, Harper pushed up from the bench.

"Where are you going?"

"Back inside to get ready for the rehearsal. I'm a bridesmaid, you know."

Sebastian stood with her. Before she could get away, he wrapped her in his arms and pulled her close to him. "I forgot to say how nice you look today."

Harper smiled. "Thank you. You don't need to lay it on so thick, though. I don't think anyone is watching us out here together."

She seemed to think that every word, every caring gesture, was part of the game when it wasn't. How was he supposed to know if anything she said or did with him was genuine? That orgasm was genuine enough, but everything else? He couldn't be sure. Perhaps the idea of something real between them was a bridge too far.

But for now, he was going to go with it.

"I don't really care," he said, dipping his head and capturing her lips in a kiss.

As rehearsed, Harper marched down the rose-petal-strewed aisle in her lavender bridesmaid gown clutching a bundle of purple-and-cream roses with dark purple freesia and ranunculus in her hands. She was the last of the bridesmaids, with the rest of the wedding party already waiting up front with the minister.

Today, the Markree Castle gallery was acting as the chapel where the wedding was taking place. The long hall was lined with wooden paneling and pale blue-green walls. As she made her way down the long stretch of chairs that lined the aisle, she looked up to the pitched wood-beam ceiling and the intricate stained-glass windows that adorned the far end of the chapel, taking in their beauty.

Turning to the left, she lined up with Emma and Lucy to await the arrival of Violet in her wedding finery. She glanced over at the groomsmen across the aisle. They all looked handsome in their black tuxedos and lavender ties. Even little Knox had a matching tux. Aidan had managed to comb his wild red hair into submission for the special occasion. He was practically beaming with his eyes laser-focused on the back of the hall for the arrival of his bride.

The musical crescendo started and all the guests stood. The doors opened and Violet stepped through on the arm of her father. Even knowing what the dress looked like on Violet, Harper still felt the magnificence steal her breath as everything came together so beautifully.

The Pnina Tornai gown from Kleinfeld's was a beautiful but relatively plain gown from the front, allowing Violet's beauty to shine. It was a strapless, white ball gown with a crystal belt and corset top that molded to her perfectly. Her neck was as long and graceful as a swan's with her hair up and a simple diamond-and-pearl choker at her throat. In her hands, she carried a magnificent hand-crafted brooch bouquet made of silk rosettes in different shades of purple and covered in Swarovski crystal pins in two dozen different styles. Dripping from the teardrop-shaped bouquet were strings of pearls and strands of crystals.

But that was just the beginning. Harper heard the gasps of the guests as Violet passed and the back of the dress was revealed. That was where the beauty of the gown shone. From the waist down, the dress was a waterfall of large, silk roses that cascaded to the floor several feet behind her. The moment Violet had put on the dress at the bridal salon, they'd all known it was the one. Few other dresses could stand up to the grand venue like this one could.

As she looked out, Harper spotted Sebastian in the crowd. He'd chosen to sit on Aidan's side since he had fewer guests attending.

He was looking incredibly dapper in his tuxedo. He claimed he hardly ever wore it, but it fit perfectly and suited him well. The only thing missing were his cufflinks that had been stolen. She had gone that afternoon to Oliver's room and borrowed a pair, claiming Sebastian had forgotten to pack his own.

Unlike everyone else in the church, whose eyes were on Violet, Sebastian's eyes were on Harper. When he realized she had turned his way, he smiled and gave her a wink before looking over to Violet with the others as she stepped up to stand beside Aidan.

Harper handed her bouquet off to Lucy so she could straighten Violet's train and veil. Once they were perfect for pictures, she took the very heavily jeweled bouquet so Violet could hold Aidan's hands during the ceremony.

Once the service began, Harper looked down at the beautiful arrangement in her hands and the reality of the moment finally hit her. She was the last of her single friends. Practically, she'd known that. Violet and Aidan had been engaged for a while as they'd planned the event, so it's not like it had snuck up on her. But until that moment, she hadn't allowed herself to really grasp what it meant.

She was on the verge of thirty, hardly an old maid, but seeing the last of her friends pair off made a wave of sadness wash over her. Why hadn't she found someone like they had? She should be happily engaged and ready to start her life with someone, and yet here she was, basically bribing a man just to pretend to be her boyfriend at the wedding.

Her gaze drifted back to Sebastian. He was sitting in the chair, listening attentively to the service. She was so thankful he was there with her for this. Yes, it was because she had asked him to be, but she wondered what would've happened between them if things had gone differently. If he had asked her to dinner instead of her asking him on this trip…if there had been no wedding and they'd decided to go for drinks after they'd met at the store…would they have become real lovers instead of ones just for show?

In that moment she wished they were in a real relationship. Not just because she didn't want to be alone, but because she found she really cared for Sebastian. He was smart, handsome, thoughtful and kind. He was there for her when she needed someone. There was a part of her that was extremely susceptible to being treated the way he treated her. That part of her wanted to fall head over heels for him.

The other part didn't know where they stood.

Yes, they had crossed the line of their fake relationship that afternoon in their room, but their ruse had muddied the water. Was their attraction real or did they just think they were into one another because they spent all day flirting and pretending to be a couple? She was pretty certain that her draw to Sebastian was authentic. The moment she'd laid eyes on him outside Neiman Marcus, she'd been attracted to his dark eyes and strong jaw. She'd wanted to know more about him instantly.

Honestly, after spending a week together, Harper found that she still wanted to know more about him. Mainly because he wasn't opening up to her the way she'd hoped. In all their conversations there had been plenty of chances for him to tell her about his childhood or where he'd grown up. His time in college. Anything outside of work. But that was really all he spoke about. His work was his life.

She knew Sebastian was passionate about his job, but she couldn't help but feel that there was more to him that he wasn't sharing. Intentionally. That worried her. Not because he was keeping potentially damaging secrets that would run her off, but because he didn't think he could open up to her.

If he didn't think he could share with her, what would happen once they returned to New York and didn't have a wedding packed full of events to get through? Would he call her? Would he want to kiss her again? Or would he return to his lab and disappear into his tools and toys the way he had before the trip?

She didn't know the answer. And that uncertainty scared her. Perhaps because no matter what the answer was, she knew it was already too late for her. Those dark eyes and that crooked smile had already captured her heart.

Maybe it wasn't being the last single friend that was troubling her today. Being single hadn't really ever bothered her before. Maybe it was knowing that, yes, she wanted a romantic moment like this for herself, but that she wanted it *with Sebastian*. She wanted him to be the man to whom she recited her vows to love, honor and cherish. She was upset because she knew deep down that she would never have this moment with him.

The loud sound of applause jerked Harper out of her thoughts. She turned to the altar in time to realize that the wedding ceremony had ended. Aidan and Violet were sharing their first kiss as husband and wife.

"Ladies and gentlemen, may I present for the very first time, Mr. and Mrs. Aidan Murphy!"

Violet turned to Harper to get her bouquet and face the crowd of wedding guests. Harper moved behind the bride to straighten her dress and veil one last time before Aidan scooped up Knox in his arms and they marched down the aisle as a family. Once they departed, she took her bouquet from Lucy.

Lucy followed the bouquet with a tissue she'd tucked away in her bra. "Here," she said, despite fighting tears of her own. "Don't mess up your makeup before the photos."

It wasn't until that moment that Harper realized she was crying. But it wasn't because of the beautiful service—it was because she knew she was right about her future with Sebastian. She dabbed her eyes, took a deep breath and pasted a smile on her face for the cameras.

No matter what, she still had a wedding reception to get through.

The new Mr. and Mrs. Aidan Murphy walked down the aisle together, holding their adorable toddler. Both of them were beaming with happiness and it took everything she had to not scowl at them as they went by. She put a fake smile on her face and clutched her program as the rest of the wedding party followed in their wake.

First was tech heiress Emma and her rebellious, gaming CEO husband, Jonah. The two of them were so beautiful together that she already hated their daughter. She was still a baby, but she would no doubt grow up to be a Victoria's Secret Angel or something. Behind them was the formerly poor but incredibly lucky Lucy, who'd managed to inherit half a billion dollars from her boss, then married her boss's nephew, Oliver, with his computer empire. She wished she'd had that kind of luck, but she'd learned she had to take control of her own destiny.

Last down the aisle was Harper on the arm of a groomsman that must be a friend of Aidan's because she didn't know him. She'd only studied the people with enough money to matter on this trip. This guy didn't matter. None of these people really did. Once she got her money, she was pretty sure she'd never see the likes of most of them again. That is, unless she uncovered another scandalous tidbit to make some more money off of them.

The guests at the wedding stood and started filing out of the gallery toward the dining hall for the cocktail reception. After thirty minutes of that overly romantic ceremony, she needed a drink. Maybe two. Or four by the time dinner rolled around. This was going to be a long night.

They were headed back to the States soon and she

could feel time was running short. Time in Ireland. Time with all of these people. Time to execute her plan and make off with the money she needed.

The blackmail payment was supposed to be at the front desk before the reception ended, but she wasn't holding her breath. Every other deadline had passed with disappointment. Why would this one be any different?

She wanted her money. She didn't want to have to pull the trigger and expose Harper. That wouldn't do either of them any good. No, Harper was being obstinate, insisting she couldn't pay when they were surrounded by people who could just write a check for that amount if they wanted to. Harper only had to ask. But she wouldn't.

Harper was going to ruin things for her. So that meant that she had no choice but to ruin things for Harper.

Nine

Sebastian spun Harper on the dance floor and then pulled her tightly against him. Dinner had been excellent, but he couldn't wait to take Harper out for a spin. He wasn't much of a dancer, but it was the only socially acceptable way he knew of to hold her body against his in public.

"You really look beautiful tonight, Harper. Have I said that yet?"

"No," she said with a smile, "but thank you. You should know, though, that I'm just a bridesmaid, so I can only be pretty. At a wedding, only the bride can be beautiful. It's the rules."

He leaned in to her and the scent of her floral perfume tickled at his nose, putting his nerves on high alert. It made him want to pull her closer. Or better yet, to tug her off the dance floor and head upstairs to their hotel room. His medical restrictions on sexual activity should be over now. He'd take it slow just in case, but he needed to indulge in Harper at least once before all of this came to an end.

Sebastian pressed his lips to the outer shell of her ear. "Well, don't tell Violet, but I think you're the most stunning woman here tonight. I don't care who the bride is. You take my breath away even when you're wearing that ugly purple dress she picked for all of you."

When he pulled away, he could see Harper blush before she glanced down to look at her dress with a critical eye. "You don't like my dress? I like it. I mean, I like it for a bridesmaid's dress. I wouldn't wear it to the Met Gala or anything, but it's pretty enough."

He didn't know what one would wear to the Met Gala, but he was pretty sure this pale purple frock with flowers on the shoulder wasn't it. "To be honest, I think you would look much prettier without it."

Her brow arched in suspicion. "I think you just want me to be naked."

Sebastian shrugged. "If you want to look your best, my vote is for naked."

"Just like a man," she groaned. "No respect for the power of fashion."

That was true. For all his money, Sebastian didn't

know one designer from the next, nor did he care. He'd be just as happy buying all his clothes at Target, if Finn would let him. He was more about function than style most days. He couldn't even tell you the name of the designer he was wearing right now. It was someone important. Finn had made sure of that. But without slipping out of his jacket to look at the name sewn inside, he had no clue.

What he did know was that the tuxedo was getting hot. Or maybe it was dancing so close to Harper that was overheating him. Looking around, he spied a door that opened onto a courtyard.

"You want to get some air? It's getting a little warm in here."

Harper glanced around the room for a moment and nodded. "Sure. I think we still have a little time before they cut the cake."

Sebastian took her hand and led her off the dance floor. They made their way around a few tables before they reached the door that opened up to the courtyard. Out there, half a dozen small bistro tables and chairs had been set up. Each table was decorated with a floral arrangement and a flickering pillar candle protected from the breeze with a tall hurricane glass. At the moment, no one was outside, giving them some privacy.

He stepped over to the stone wall that separated the patio from the gardens beyond. It was a clear, cool night with a sky full of stars. He couldn't imagine this many stars existed if he lived in Manhattan his whole life. He'd only seen this many on nights in Maine as a kid. Even so, it hardly held a candle to the beauty of the woman standing beside him.

He hadn't just been flattering her earlier, it was the truth. It would be so easy in a moment like this— with candlelight highlighting the soft curves of her face and stars reflecting in her eyes—to let his guard down and fall for Harper once and for all. The music and the moonlight seemed to be conspiring against him tonight, wearing down his defenses. This week was supposed to be relaxing and yet he'd spent the entire trip fighting with himself.

He hadn't expected any of this when he'd agreed to come to Ireland. Yes, he'd thought he would spend a few days holding hands with and kissing a beautiful woman overseas. He'd never imagined that he would be tempted to take their fake relationship seriously and open up to her. That he might look forward to returning to New York and spending time with her instead of rushing back into his lab at the first opportunity.

If he had, he might not have taken the trip. His work was at such a critical point. Could he risk taking time away to build something serious with Harper? He wasn't sure.

"Ahh, this feels good," Harper said. "Normally it would be cold, but it got so hot in the ballroom."

"Maybe it's all the champagne," Sebastian offered.

"Or maybe it's the pressure," she said with a sigh.

"Pressure? What kind of pressure?"

Harper leaned her elbows against the patio wall to look out at the garden. "The reception will be over soon and my time is running out. That means the blackmailer is going to realize he isn't going to get any more money out of me. He won't have any choice but to expose my secret. I wonder how long he'll wait. Will he reveal the truth tonight? Wait until the morning and ruin my flight home? Maybe wait until we're back in New York and have something printed in the paper so everyone, not just the wedding guests, finds out? I wish I knew how it would happen so I could brace myself for it."

Sebastian had been enjoying the romantic evening with Harper and pondering a future with her, and all the while her mind was on her troubles instead of her company. Perhaps he'd better put those thoughts aside before he regretted them. "And here I thought you might be enjoying the wedding reception."

She shook her head sadly and straightened up. "I wish I could. This was supposed to be a great trip and a special wedding for one of my best friends. Instead it's been nothing but a waking nightmare where everyone has Irish accents. I really just want to get on the plane and go home so I can get started dealing with the fallout."

Sebastian took her hand in his. She felt so small and delicate in his grip when she was speaking in such a defeated tone. "You're going to be okay, you know."

"What do you mean?"

"I mean that no matter what happens, you're a strong, independent woman. You've made the best of your situation before and you'll continue to make the best of it, regardless of what the blackmailer does. He might feel like he's in control of your fate, but he's really not. How you handle your situation is entirely up to you."

Harper studied his face for a moment and nodded. "You're right. And I think I'm going to start handling the situation right now." She turned away from him to head back into the reception.

Sebastian reached out and grasped her wrist before she could get away. "Wait. What are you going to do?"

She took a deep breath and straightened her spine. "I'm going to confront Quentin and put an end to this."

"Quentin? May I speak with you privately for a moment?"

He hesitated, looking at his fiancée before whispering into her ear and nodding to Harper.

Harper hadn't had any discussions with Jessie or Josie or Jamie—whatever her name was. She wasn't interested in chatting with her ex-boyfriend's new fiancée. It was hard enough to look at the glittering diamond rock on her ring finger and not think about the bare finger on her own hand. The only difference lately was that when she imagined a man down on one knee proposing, there was only one face that came to mind.

And it sure wasn't Quentin's.

He finally disentangled himself from his fiancée and followed Harper out into the hallway. "What's this all about, Harper? Josie doesn't really like me talking to you, to be honest. The sooner I'm back in the reception, the better off I'll be."

Harper couldn't care less about Quentin's fiancée and her jealous streak. "This won't take long. All I want to say is that I can't give you any more money, Quentin."

She'd hoped that her blunt confrontation would catch him off guard and he might give something away. Instead he stopped short and narrowed his gaze at her. "What are you talking about, Harper?"

She crossed her arms over her chest. "Oh, cut it out. I'm tired of playing these games, *B. Mayler.* I've given you all the money I can get my hands on right now. You've stolen jewelry from my room and that will have to suffice until—"

"Wait," Quentin said, holding up his hands. "I haven't stolen anything from your room. I don't even know where your room is in this place. And what money? Seriously, Harper, I have no idea what you're talking about."

Her ex's tone gave her pause. It was a sincerely

confused voice and it matched the expression on his face. "You're being sued, right? And your dad cut you off, didn't he?"

A ruddy blush of embarrassment came to his cheeks. "How did you hear about all that?"

"It's a small world. But I know it's true, so don't pretend you don't need the money."

"Sure, I could use some money. I wouldn't have dropped fifty grand on Josie's ring if I knew my dad was going to cut me loose a few weeks later. He doesn't like Josie, but I'm sure he and I will work that out. And the lawsuit is no big deal. My attorneys are handling it. But I don't know what my problems have to do with you."

"You're going to stand there and tell me that you're not the one that's blackmailing me?"

"What? No, I'm not." His eyes widened in concern and he leaned closer to speak in a softer voice. "Someone is blackmailing you?"

The concern in his voice might as well have been a punch to the gut. Harper didn't know what to say or do, but the truth was plain as day when she looked into his clueless face: Quentin was not her blackmailer.

So who the hell was?

"You know what? Just forget I said anything," Harper said. "Go back inside before Josie gets upset."

Quentin hesitated for a moment and then nodded, silently returning to the reception hall.

Harper was relieved to see him go without a fight, but the relief was short-lived.

From the very first blackmail message, she'd been fairly certain that Quentin had been behind it. He was the only one with the slightest inkling of her financial difficulties. When they'd dated and she'd finally opened up about her problems, he'd actually coached her on some financial planning. They'd even used the same financial advisor. But no one else, until she'd told Sebastian, had known.

Maybe she was fooling herself. Maybe everyone saw through her ruse and was too kind to say anything. They just let her carry on as though no one was the wiser. If that was the case, then anyone could be the blackmailer.

Harper stood at the entrance to the reception hall and watched everyone enjoying themselves inside. Violet and Aidan were cutting the cake while a crowd gathered around them. Flashes from cameras and the *awws* of bystanders drew everyone to the corner where the towering confection was on display. A few people were sitting at their tables, chatting and sipping their flutes of champagne.

Some people she knew better than others, but who was capable of blackmailing her? Of ransacking her room and stealing both her and Sebastian's things? She didn't even know where to begin looking for a new suspect.

"Miss Drake?"

Harper turned her attention to the waiter who had come up beside her. He had previously been carrying a silver tray of champagne flutes, but now his tray held nothing but the miserably familiar white envelope.

"I have a message for you," he said. "It was left at the front desk."

Of course it was. "Thank you," she said with a sigh and accepted the letter. She supposed she should open it and see what the latest threat entailed. The money was due by the end of the reception. There was only an hour or so left in that and she was pretty sure that both of them knew she wasn't paying it. So what was the point?

She slipped the envelope into the front of her bra to read later. Maybe. What did it matter in the end? She wouldn't have the money. Unless the blackmailer was bluffing the whole time, her news was going to come out sooner or later.

When she'd first told Sebastian about the note she'd received on the plane, he'd told her that one of her courses of action would be to expose the truth before anyone else could. To take the power back from the blackmailer. At the time, the idea had been out of the question. She would be throwing everything out the window if she did that. Now she wondered if that hadn't been the best policy all along. Perhaps if she spoke to her grandfather and explained her situation, he would understand. Or not. Perhaps he would cut her off and that twenty-eight million would vanish into thin air.

So what?

It seemed like a ridiculous thought to have. It was a life-changing amount of money. She'd been scraping by for years waiting for the day that money would arrive. But now that she stood there, she realized that things hadn't been so terrible. She had managed just fine. She had a good job at FlynnSoft that paid well and offered amazing benefits like a gym, a no-cost cafeteria and coffee shop, and insurance for minimum premiums and co-pays. Her beautiful, large apartment was paid for. The fees and insurance were high, but she paid them every year without fail.

No, she didn't have all the latest fashions. Her high-end pieces were either relics from her previous spending days or lucky thrift store finds. She had learned over the years how to get by without keeping up with the Joneses. If she told the truth about her situation to her friends and family, the pressure to shop and spend money with them would likely go away. No one had ever treated Lucy any differently when she'd been the poor one in the group. After she'd inherited half a billion dollars and married Harper's rich brother, she was still the same old Lucy.

Perhaps she could be the same old Harper. Just a little less flashy. She'd spent the last eight years just trying to get to her thirtieth birthday when perhaps she needed to be happy that she had made it all this time on her own. If she wasn't pretending to be something she wasn't, she could make changes to make her life easier. Maybe she could sell her flashy apartment for something more reasonable, then pocket the profit into savings. She could sell some of her designer clothes that she never wore anymore.

The realization that she didn't need her grandfather's money was a profound one for her. Suddenly it was as though a great weight had been lifted from her shoulders. She didn't know who her blackmailer was, but she was about to stick it to them. The one thing they couldn't have counted on was the spoiled heiress Harper Drake having the nerve to go it on her own.

Straightening her spine, Harper marched into the reception hall with a feeling of purpose. Cake was being distributed and the happy couple was sharing a piece at their table near the front. The band was playing a soft instrumental piece and the dance floor was empty for the moment. This was her chance.

She snatched a flute of champagne from a passing server and climbed the steps of the stage. Several people had made toasts to the couple from this perch earlier. Violet had only had bridesmaids since she said she couldn't choose a maid of honor from her three best friends. Harper could easily be the next one from the wedding party to make a toast to the happy couple.

The stage band saw her approach and eased out of the song they were playing so she could offer her good wishes to the bride and groom. She nodded and waved to them, taking the microphone from the stand and walking to the edge of the platform.

"Hello, everyone. I'm Harper Drake and I've known Violet for many years. Our families knew each other growing up, but we really got close when Violet and I went to Yale together and joined the same sorority. Pi Beta Phi sisters forever!"

The crowd laughed and applauded. "It's true. There, I made best friends for life. Not just Violet, but also Emma and Lucy, who is now my sister-in-law. Over the last few years, I've seen each of these beautiful, smart, wonderful women find love and happiness. I could not be happier for all of you. And tonight, I want to raise a toast to Violet and Aidan. May your lives together always be as magical as the fairy-tale wedding where it started."

She raised her glass and the room applauded and joined her in the toast. Harper didn't leave the stage, however. She waited for the applause to die down and continued. "Tonight, in this room, are some of the most important people in my life. So I wanted you all to hear the brief announcement that I'd like to make. No—I'm not engaged or pregnant, so let's just get that out of the way," she said with a smile. "I actually want you all to know that I've been lying to you.

"Every day for the last eight years or so, I have gotten out of bed and lived a lie. I have carried on with my life as though nothing has ever changed, but the truth is that I am broke. Flat broke. It seems silly in retrospect to lie about something like that, but my pride got in the way. No accountant wants to be seen as a poor money manager and that's what I was. I was spoiled rotten and when the well ran dry, I didn't know what to do."

Harper sipped her champagne and took a moment. Her eyes stayed focused on the tapestry on the back wall. She feared that making eye contact with someone might make her start to cry and she didn't want to do that right now.

"You're probably wondering why I'm up here telling you this. It's because someone found out about my lie—someone in this very room—and they've been using it to blackmail me. You see, if my grandfather found out I wasted all my money, I would lose the rest of my inheritance. So they've harassed me throughout this entire trip. They've taken thousands from me I couldn't afford to give, ransacked my hotel suite and stolen family pieces that can never be replaced. They've demanded money that I can't pay. And I won't ever pay it because my inheritance is basically out the window at this point.

"So I'm up here tonight to tell all of you the truth and to apologize for misleading you. And also to tell my blackmailer, whomever he or she is, that they can kiss my ass. Thank you."

She put the microphone back in the stand and made her way off of the stage as quickly as possible. She had done what she'd had to do, but she wasn't sure if she was ready to face the backlash yet. The room was unnervingly quiet, but eventually the band started to play again.

"Harper!"

She heard someone shout her name, but she didn't stop. She couldn't stop. She just wanted to get out of the ballroom as quickly as she could.

Harper made it out of the party and down the hallway before she felt a warm hand clamp down on her wrist. She stopped, spinning on her heel to find Sebastian standing behind her.

"Let me go, please," she said. "I just want to go back to our room."

He looked at her with his big, dark eyes and nodded. "That's fine. But you're not going without me."

Ten

Alone in their suite, they took their time getting undressed. There was no sense of urgency pressing them on. Tonight, she knew, they were going to savor the moment. It was their last night together and an emotionally heightened one after everything that had just happened downstairs.

"Unzip me please," she asked, presenting her back to Sebastian and lifting her hair.

He had already slipped out of his jacket and tie. He approached her, gently taking the zipper and sliding it slowly down her back. Harper could feel his fingertips grazing along her spine as he traveled down to the curve of her lower back. His touch sent a shiver through her whole body. She closed her eyes to savor the sensation of his warm breath against her skin.

His large, firm hands cupped her shoulders, pushing the one floral strap down her arm. With little effort, her dress slipped to her waist and then pooled at her feet in a puddle of lavender chiffon.

She heard his sharp intake of breath and realized he had discovered her lavender lace boy shorts. She had strategically chosen them for several reasons. First, was how they would wear beneath the dress. Second was that the cut highlighted the curve of her butt nicely. And last, they were replaceable when Sebastian tore them.

She felt his fingers grip the clasp of her strapless bra and then it fell to the floor with the rest of her clothes.

"Looks like you dropped something," he said.

Harper glanced down at the floor and realized that the note from the blackmailer she'd tucked into her bra had fallen out. She bent to pick it up and held it thoughtfully in her hand. "Another love note," she said.

Without hesitation she walked across the room to the fireplace and tossed it inside. The flames immediately started to blacken and curl the corners, then the whole thing was engulfed in the orange blaze. Although she hadn't intended it to be a symbolic gesture, it felt like one now. Consequences be damned, she was done with her blackmailer.

"Now, enough of that interrupting my trip." Harper turned back to Sebastian and approached him. She started unbuttoning his dress shirt, feeling immediately calmer and content as her hands ran over the chest hair hidden beneath it. "I don't want to think about anything but you and me right now."

She pushed his shirt over his broad shoulders and then wrapped her arms around his neck. Her lips sought his out tentatively. When they met, she molded against him, pressing her breasts into the hard wall of his chest to get as close to him as she could. "Make love to me tonight," she whispered against his mouth. "I want you. All of you."

Sebastian kissed her tenderly and then pulled away. There was a hesitation in him she didn't understand, but she shoved her doubts away when he said, "Whatever you want, darling."

His words made her smile. She hooked her fingers into the loops of his pants and tugged him over to the bed. Harper sat on the edge, bringing his waist to her eye level. There, she unfastened his belt, unbuttoned and unzipped his tuxedo pants, and slipped them down with his briefs.

She reached out for him then. He was hard and ready for her without even touching. She wrapped her fingers around his soft skin and stroked gently until she heard him groan. She moved faster, leaning in to flick her tongue across the tip.

"Harper!" Sebastian nearly shouted, grasping her

wrist to still the movement. "Wait a minute," he said. "Before we... I don't have anything."

Harper leaned over to the nightstand and pulled a small box of condoms out of the drawer. "I picked these up when we were in town one day."

After their last encounter, she'd wondered if not having protection had put the brakes on things and she hadn't wanted to run into that problem again.

The breath rushed out of his lungs all at once. "Oh, thank you," he groaned. With that worry off his mind, Sebastian seemed to become more engaged. He pressed Harper back against the pillows and covered her body with his.

She loved the feel of his weight holding her down, the scent of his cologne and skin teasing her nose, and the heat of him warming her chilled body. His lips and hands were all over her, leaving no inch of skin unloved as he moved lower and lower down her body.

His fingers brushed over the lace barrier between them. To her surprise, he eased them from her hips and tossed them to the side. "I like those," he said when he caught her surprised expression. "If I ruin them, you can't wear them again."

Harper laughed, but the sound was trapped in her throat when his fingers dipped between her thighs and stroked her center. Instead it came out a strangled cry as he knowingly teased the right spot. When his finger slipped inside her, Harper's inner muscles clamped down and both of them groaned aloud.

"I wanted to take my time with this," he said, shaking his head.

She reached for the condoms and handed him the box. "We can take our time later. I want you right now. I'm ready."

"So am I." He didn't hesitate to tear open the box and grab one of the foil packets from inside. Within seconds Sebastian had the latex rolled down his length and in place.

Harper shifted her legs to cradle him between her thighs and slid her hips lower.

He leaned forward, bracing himself on his elbows.

Harper lifted her knees to wrap them around his hips, but he stopped, leaning down to kiss her instead. "Thank you," he whispered.

"For what?"

"For this week. I know I was supposed to be helping you, but I needed this time away almost as much as I need you. So thank you for that." Sebastian kissed her again and this time he pressed his hips forward and entered her, ending any further conversation.

Harper gasped against his lips as Sebastian filled her. She gripped his face in her hands and kissed him hard even as he eased back and surged forward into her again. She was surprised by the stirring of pleasure deep inside her. It wasn't something she expected based on past experience, but there was something about the way he moved. A tilt of his hips, maybe, that made every stroke more amazing than the last in a way she couldn't even describe. It was just like Sebastian to have mastered the mechanics of sex.

It was so intense, she had no choice but to close her eyes and hold on. She clung to his bare back and lifted her hips to meet his every advance. Her cries grew louder and louder as her release built inside her and she couldn't hold back any longer. She shouted his name as the dam broke and the rush of pleasure surged through her.

He thrust harder then. Previously his movements had been controlled and measured in a way that was distinctly Sebastian. He seemed to be taking his time and yet ensuring every stroke made the maximum impact. As her orgasm started to fade, she realized the calculated Sebastian was giving way to a man on the edge.

He thrust hard, again and again, until he finally stiffened and groaned in her ear. He held perfectly still for a moment, his eyes squeezed tightly shut. Then he collapsed beside her on the mattress, his breath ragged with strain.

Harper curled up against his side, resting her head on his chest to listen to his heartbeat, which was faster than she expected. They lay together like that until both his breathing and his pulse had slowed to normal. At that point, he seemed to relax.

He wrapped his arm around her and placed a kiss against her forehead.

"Everything okay?" she asked, lifting her head to look up at him.

"Yes, we're good," he said. "Great, actually."

Harper chuckled and lay back. "I'm glad. I've been fantasizing about this moment all week."

"Really?" Sebastian laughed. "I'm sorry to make you hold out so long. I figured you had other things on your mind. Speaking of which, you were really amazing tonight."

"Well, thank you. I aim to please."

Sebastian swatted her bottom playfully. "That's not what I meant. I was talking about the reception. It took a lot of guts to get up there and take control of your situation. I was really proud of you."

"Oh," she said in a sheepish tone.

"What prompted it? You went to talk to Quentin and the next thing I know, you're on stage."

"I spoke with him, but it was apparent that he wasn't involved. That scared me. I had no idea who I could be dealing with and I decided it wasn't worth hiding any longer. You had been right from the beginning—exposing myself was the only way to take back my power. But I don't want to talk about that anymore. It's taken up this whole trip and I want to put it behind me. Tonight I'd rather talk about you for a change."

She felt Sebastian stiffen in her arms at the mention of talking about him. "Please," she added. "Tell me something I don't know about you. Like why you decided to go into medical technology. What inspired you? And I don't mean whatever practiced answer you put together for the company web site. The truth. What happened?"

He'd spoken about combining his engineering skills with Finn's medical expertise before and it seemed a winning combination, but there was still more to it. She could tell. No one dedicated themselves to their work like that without a reason. A personal reason.

Sebastian sat thoughtfully for a moment. The silence was long enough for her to worry he might not answer. But then he began.

"I was a shy, nerdy sort of kid. I liked to tinker. My older brother, Kenny, was more outdoorsy. He was always riding his bike or skateboarding. He stayed active."

Harper felt anxiety start to tighten her shoulders. She should've anticipated that this conversation wouldn't be a cheerful one. With his type of work, inspiration likely came from some kind of tragedy. She wanted to kick herself and yet, in the moment, was so grateful he was sharing, she would happily listen to any story he told.

"His best friend in high school ended up getting a four-wheeler for his birthday one year. My brother had graduated from high school at that point and he and a couple friends had gone camping somewhere to ride the ATV and hang out for the weekend. I don't know the details of what happened, but Kenny ended up rolling the four-wheeler. He was wearing a helmet, thankfully, but the ATV landed on top of him and crushed his lower spine. They were so deep in the woods, they couldn't land a helicopter out there to get him, so they had to carry him out on a gurney until they could reach an ambulance, which drove him to a place where the helicopter could pick him up."

Harper grasped his hand in the dark as he spoke, squeezing it tightly.

"The accident severed his spinal cord. He was eighteen and doomed to be a paraplegic for the rest of his life. I saw the toll his accident took on him and on my family. It was my hope that doing the work I do, someday I could develop something that would help him. One of the projects I've worked on for years has been a mechanical exoskeleton that would allow Kenny to walk again."

"That sounds amazing."

"It does. But so far, it's been the one thing that has eluded me. I have the technology together. I have a prototype that works in the lab. But my goal is to create something anyone can afford. Not just for rich people or ones with good insurance. That is going to take more time. That's why I work so much. For Kenny. And all the other Kennys in the world."

Harper had asked the question and now she knew

the answer. In that moment she almost wished she hadn't. Now she knew just how important his work was to him. It was personal. It was his first love. Unlike Quentin, who used his work as a cover for affairs, Sebastian was truly a workaholic. It made her wonder if that meant there would never be any room in his life for anything—or anyone—else.

It was then that she realized that she was fighting a losing battle with him. No matter what happened between them, she could never fully have Sebastian in her life. She would be better served by keeping her feelings to herself and moving on once they arrived home.

There was someone out there for Harper. Someone who would love her, treat her well and let her be the most important thing in his life. Unfortunately that man just wasn't Sebastian West.

"Ladies and gentleman, welcome to New York. The current time is nine thirty in the evening."

Sebastian perked up in his seat after the wheels hit the ground and the pilot announced the long flight was finally over. He wished he'd been able to sleep on the way back and have it go as quickly as flying over, but that wasn't the way it worked.

Instead he'd spent most of the flight watching the television in the lounge with several other wedding guests. Harper had been…quiet…since they'd left Ireland. He wasn't sure what was wrong. Things had to be looking up. The blackmailer was out of business, they didn't have to pretend to be dating any longer, they were back home…life could return to normal.

Even Sebastian was relieved to know he only had a few days left on his leave before he could get back into the office. He might not burst through the door like usual, but he had a lot of exciting sketches in his notebook and he was ready to get to work on the prototypes as soon as possible.

Perhaps Harper wasn't interested in things returning to normal. Going home meant facing the consequences of her actions with her grandfather. Even Sebastian had to admit that he wasn't quite ready for their fake relationship to come to an end. But she hadn't voiced any interest in continuing. Perhaps he had read too much into their physical connection.

They were two of the last people off the plane. Most everyone had their drivers picking them up in black, luxury sedans, so the parking lot of the small airport emptied quickly. By the time they collected their bags and went out to where they'd parked, Sebastian found it was just the two of them.

"So now what?" he asked, setting down his luggage beside his car. Although he rarely drove it in the city, he had a blue BMW that he traveled back and forth to Maine in from time to time.

Harper set her bag down and sighed. "I've got an Uber coming to get me."

"That's not what I meant," he said. "I meant with us."

She crossed her arms over her chest in a defensive posture she'd never taken with him before. "I don't know. The week is over. Thank you very much for being my boyfriend on the trip. You were very… thorough."

"Thorough?" He couldn't keep the irritation from his voice. "Is that what you call it?"

"What else would you call it, Sebastian?"

There was a tone in her voice that he couldn't pinpoint. He wasn't sure if she was daring him to admit that it was more than just for show or not. Did she want him to profess his undying love and beg her to be his girlfriend for real? Or did she just want him to lay out his feelings so she could stomp on them? The way she'd pulled away from him today made him unsure.

"I sure as hell wouldn't—"

"Your time is up, Miss Drake," a woman's voice interrupted him.

Both Harper and Sebastian turned their attention to the shadowy figure standing in the dark, empty parking lot outside the airport.

The person took a few steps closer into the beam of an overhead light and Sebastian could finally make out who was standing there.

He didn't know her name, but he recognized the woman as Quentin's fiancée. And more importantly, she was aiming a gun at Harper.

Without thinking, he took a step forward and put his arm out to shield Harper. "What the hell are you doing pointing a gun at people?" he asked.

"Josie?" Harper asked from over his shoulder. "What's going on?"

"Surprised?" The woman smiled but it came out more like a smirk. "I bet you didn't suspect little old me for a second, did you? Of course not. You haven't given me a second thought this whole trip. I wasn't important or rich like the rest of you. I was just the disposable arm candy."

That was true. Sebastian had hardly paid any attention to the younger woman who'd always seemed glued to Quentin's side. To be fair, he hadn't really known many of the people on the trip, but Josie had been a silent, ignorable presence. Harper hadn't even known the woman and she knew everybody.

If that was true, how had Josie managed to get hold of such personal, private information about Harper?

"You're the one blackmailing me?"

"Guilty," Josie said without moving the gun a centimeter. It was still fixed on Harper, even if it had to go through Sebastian to get there.

"I don't understand," Harper said, pushing his arm out of the way. "How did you find out about my trust conditions? Did Quentin tell you?"

Josie shook her head. "All Quentin provided me was access to you. The rest I got on my own. If you'd bothered to speak to me this trip, you might've discovered that I work for your financial management firm. I know everything about you, Harper, including the provisions of your trust. I just knew a spoiled diva like you would've blown it. It only took a little digging to find out what I needed to know. Honestly, it was too easy."

"Why would you do this to me, Josie? I've never done anything to you."

"Aww, it wasn't personal, Harper. It's just about the money. It could've just as easily been any one of you."

"It was personal to me. Ransacking our room? Taking my late mother's necklace, his grandfather's watch—that was personal. I've spent the last week tied in knots because of you. And for what? Just some money?"

"You say that just like a rich person. You've gotten good at fooling everyone. Yes, I just did it for some money. That's enough for most people, although I have to admit I haven't gotten much cash out of the deal. I've spent this whole trip trying to get my point across with you, but nothing seems to be working. I've threatened you, stalked you, raised the price, promised to expose you, and here I stand with mere pennies of what you owe me."

"I don't owe you anything. Nobody owes you a damn thing. Everything you've gotten was taken by force."

"And everything you've gotten was given to you on a silver platter. All you have to do is give me the money and I'll be on my way."

"You of all people know that I won't have any money until after my birthday. How can I pay you what I don't have?"

Sebastian wished he could think of something to do. Like some smooth kung-fu move to kick the gun out of Josie's hand and then wrestle her to the ground. But he was an engineer. At best, he could outthink her. If he could get his heart to stop pounding so loudly so he could focus.

"Like you couldn't get it if you needed it with all your rich and powerful friends. Violet spent more money on the rehearsal dinner alone than I was asking for. To tell the truth, I feel like I've been accommodating. I doubt there are many other blackmailers out there that would've given you as many chances as I have, Harper. But I'm done being nice. I need the money and I need it now."

"Why would I pay you another cent?" Harper asked. "It's all over, Josie. It's been over since the wedding. Everyone knows my secret. You can't blackmail me with it anymore."

She nodded. "That's true. That's why I brought along the gun. This isn't so much a blackmailing anymore as an armed robbery. I want my money."

"Why do you need money from me? You're marrying Quentin. His family has plenty of money. A hundred thousand is nothing to them."

"And I'm nothing to Quentin," Josie replied with narrowed eyes. "It turns out he was just using me to make you jealous. He proposed and brought me on this trip just because he knew it would bother you. He never expected daddy to cut him off in the process. Now that the trip is over and he sees you're in love with someone else, he's dropped me like a rock and gone crawling back for forgiveness. So the money is more important than ever, actually."

Sebastian watched the heated discussion continue to volley between the two women. He curled his hands into fists at his sides as frustration and anger built inside him, but he felt an unpleasant tingling sensation running down his left arm. It forced him to shake out his hand in the hope it would go away.

It didn't.

The women continued to talk, but he found he couldn't focus on their words any longer. He felt the panic start to rise in him. Yes, Josie was holding a gun on them, but this was a different kind of panic. A familiar one. He was getting dizzy as he tried to focus on the two small figures standing in front of him. He reached out for Harper to steady himself before he stumbled.

"Sebastian!" Harper said in a startled voice. "What's wrong? Are you okay?" she asked.

He wanted to answer her but he couldn't. His chest

was suddenly so tight he could barely breathe, much less speak. As the vise tightened harder on his rib cage, he realized that this wasn't just some random panic attack. This was another heart attack—a stronger one than last time.

The doctors had warned him to take it easy. And he'd tried. He'd done as best he was able and yet here he was—looking into the eyes of the woman he loved and wondering if it was for the last time. Was it done? Had he lost his chance to say all the things to Harper he'd been too afraid to voice? Could he say enough in time?

"I love…" He gasped and hunched over, unable to finish. His hand slipped from her shoulder and he heard her scream as his knees buckled beneath him.

Blackness enveloped Sebastian and he was unconscious before he hit the hard pavement.

Eleven

"Harper?"

Harper sat up from a dead sleep, making the best she could out of the recliner in Sebastian's hospital room. Still groggy, she wiped an unfortunate bit of drool from her chin and looked around. That's when she realized that Sebastian was awake.

She leaped from the chair to stand at his bedside. "You're up," she said with a smile.

"I guess. I feel like I've been hit by a truck." He brought his hand up to his face, dragging all his IV tubes along with it. "What happened? Where am I?"

Harper was surprised but relieved that he didn't remember the last few days. It had been a roller coaster of tests, bloodwork, scans and, finally, a stint placed in one of the arteries to his heart. He'd been out of it most of the time. Harper had just sat by his bedside waiting for the next bit of news from the nurses and doctors caring for him.

"You had a heart attack at the airport," Harper explained. "You've been in the hospital for a couple of days."

Sebastian frowned as he looked around, taking inventory of his body. "Why does my wrist hurt?"

"That's how they went in to put a stint in your chest."

He put his hand against his chest and shook his head. "Wow."

Harper sat on the edge of the bed. She'd been filled with a mix of emotions over the last few days that she'd never expected—and never wanted to experience again. First was the fear of being shot by a vengeful and bitter Josie. She'd never anticipated being confronted with a weapon like that and had hardly known how to respond. When Sebastian collapsed, Harper had reacted and rushed to his side, forgetting all about Josie. She wasn't sure how long her blackmailer had stood there with the gun, but eventually Harper looked up and Josie was gone. Apparently she hadn't wanted to hang around for the fire department and ambulance to arrive.

Since then, she'd hardly given that situation any thought. The fear of suddenly losing Sebastian before she could tell him how she felt had taken its place in her mind. All the way to the hospital, she'd sat in the back of the ambulance, racked with guilt at thinking she'd put him in a dangerous situation that had almost killed him. Then days of anxiety waiting for the results of all his tests.

Finally, and most recently, she was angry.

That was the most surprising emotion, but the one she couldn't shake. The night before, the doctor who had been treating Sebastian had come in with another man he introduced as Sebastian's cardiologist. They'd spoken to her about his ongoing condition like it was something she was aware of. They'd discussed how this was more serious than his previous attack. Two weeks away from the office wouldn't be enough this time.

As they'd continued, it became harder for her to keep a neutral expression on her face. Harper hadn't wanted them to know she had no idea what they were talking about. But the more they'd talked, the more things about Sebastian had started to fall into place.

Like why the workaholic could drop everything and take a trip to Ireland. He wasn't *allowed* to work. Not after his last heart attack had driven him to the floor of his lab less than two weeks ago.

Two weeks ago he'd had a heart attack and he hadn't said anything about it. He'd acted like nothing happened and got on a plane with her to Ireland. The truth of it made her mind spin. What if something had happened in Ireland? That castle had been out in the middle of nowhere, literally hours from Dublin. How long would it have taken to get him to a hospital with a state-of-the-art cardiac care unit?

If he had told her, at least she could've known to watch for the signs. Or when he'd collapsed, she would have known what it was and been able to tell the 9-1-1 operator and the EMTs he had a heart condition. As it was, she'd just sat helplessly, crying and saying, "He just collapsed," over and over in despair and confusion.

Talking to his business partner hadn't made her feel any better. Finn was listed as his emergency contact and medical power of attorney, so he'd been called into the hospital the minute they'd arrived. He was the one who had authorized the tests and cleared it with the hospital for Harper to stay even when she wasn't family. She was indebted to Finn for that alone, much less the information he'd shared with her while he was there.

"The doctors said you're going to be okay. But you've got to take it easy. You'll probably be discharged tomorrow. Finn has set up a nurse to stay with you at your apartment."

"I don't need a nurse," he argued.

"Finn says, and I agree, that you lost your ability to make decisions in this arena when you had that second attack. You're not going into work. You're getting a nurse to make sure you're taking all the medications and eating well. You're supposed to register for a cardiac rehabilitation program to help you rebuild your stamina and design an exercise regime to keep this from happening again. You have to do it all, to the letter, or you're going to have another attack. You might not bounce back the next time."

Sebastian opened his mouth to argue with her and then stopped himself. "Okay. You're right."

Harper had practiced what she'd wanted to say to him a few times in her mind. She wasn't sure it would come out right, but she had to try anyway. "It's been a long couple of days in this hospital, Sebastian."

"I bet. Weren't you wearing that outfit on the flight home?"

Harper looked down, but she knew he was right. She hadn't gone home. She had ventured down to the gift shop for a toothbrush and some other toiletries to get her through, but other than that, she hadn't left his side. Their suitcases and everything in them had been left behind at the airport where they'd run into Josie. In the ambulance, she'd called Jonah and he'd gone back to pick up their things for them. He and Emma had offered to bring her whatever she'd needed, but she hadn't wanted to be a bigger imposition than she'd already been.

"It's been even more stressful for me because it came out of the blue. Young, healthy thirty-eight-year-old men do not just drop to the ground with a heart attack, Sebastian."

She watched as his jaw tightened. "I didn't think it was important."

"Important?" she cried. "You didn't think it was important to tell me that you were recovering from a heart attack? That you were supposed to be recuperating? I didn't need to know that because *it wasn't important*? We had sex, Sebastian. That could've killed you."

Sebastian sighed. "I didn't want you to treat me like I was fragile. I'm not fragile. The sex didn't kill me. Not even close. And if that woman hadn't tried to kill us, I probably wouldn't even be here right now."

"That's not what the doctor said. He said that you were supposed to schedule a heart catheterization while you were off from work to check for arterial blockages. Not only did you not schedule it, you left the country instead. You could've died, Sebastian. Right there at my feet. And I wouldn't have had the slightest clue as to what was happening to you or why because you didn't tell me."

"I thought I had it handled. I didn't want to worry you when you had your own problems to deal with."

"If it were only that, I might buy it. But it's more than just your heart condition, Sebastian. Yes, you kept something so important a secret from me, but you haven't opened up to me about anything else, either."

"I told you about my brother."

She nodded. "Only as it pertained to your work

and your inspiration. You never share anything about your past, your feelings. You just won't let me in."

That was the crux of it: how could he possibly care about her—really, truly care about her—if he was shutting her out like this?

It was then she realized that maybe this was a problem of her own making. This wasn't supposed to be a real relationship, despite how far they'd gone off the rails. They weren't supposed to confide in each other, get physical and fall in love. She was the one who'd broken the rules and fallen for him. She'd poured her heart and soul out to him and gotten nothing in return. So this was really a mess she'd made. She couldn't be mad at him for sticking to their agreement. He didn't love her. And she had to be okay with that.

But she didn't need to stay around and witness the evidence of her foolishness any longer. If she stayed, she would say something she would regret and she didn't want to agitate him any more than she already had when he was in this fragile state.

"Where are you going?" he asked as she stood and scooped her purse up from the floor.

"I'm going home."

"Why?"

Harper stopped and looked at him one last time. "Because the wedding is over," she said. "Thanks for pretending to be my date this week. I couldn't have gotten through it all without you."

He sat up in the bed and reached for her. "Wait. Are you coming back?"

She moved toward the door, finally shaking her head. "Why would I? Now I know you're going to be okay. You're in good hands. Goodbye, Sebastian." She slipped out the door before he could respond.

Dashing down the hallway, she rushed into the nearest elevator to keep from changing her mind.

"Mr. West, you have a visitor," Ingrid called from the living room.

Sebastian had heard the phone ring a few minutes earlier and assumed it was the front desk. They were the only ones who called the house line. That meant he either had a delivery coming up or a visitor. He'd already received some flowers from his parents and a plant from work, so he'd figured there might be a guest coming upstairs. He had gotten out of bed, put on some real clothes and straightened his disheveled appearance in anticipation of company.

Looking in the mirror was rough. His goatee was getting long and the rest of his beard was starting to fill in with coarse, almost black hair since he hadn't shaved since in Ireland. He needed a haircut, too, as the dark waves were getting wild and fighting his comb to stay standing straight. His eyes were bloodshot and he was bruised and scabby from the elbows down from the hospital using him as a human pin cushion.

It really was a lost cause. A brush through his hair and a swig of mouthwash was the best he could do on short notice. He wanted to look somewhat put together just in case it was Harper.

He'd had a couple visitors since he'd gotten home from the hospital—his family had even driven down from Maine to see him—but the only person he really wanted to see was Harper. So far, she had eluded him.

He made his way down the hallway to where his home health aide, Ingrid, was waiting on him. She smiled and gestured to the couch where someone was sitting. It was Finn.

Damn.

"Don't get too excited to see me," Finn said in a dry tone. "I wouldn't want to put too much strain on your heart."

Sebastian made his way over to his recliner next to the couch and settled into it.

Ingrid brought them both bottles of sparkling water and then disappeared into the kitchen to give them some privacy.

"Sorry," Sebastian said. "I was hoping you were someone else."

"Harper, perhaps?"

"Yes." There was no sense in trying to deny it.

"Has she been by to see you since you left the hospital?"

"No." It had been several long, lonely days without her smiling face and sassy attitude.

Finn frowned at his partner. "That seems odd. Are you sure that she's okay? She wouldn't leave your side for a moment at the hospital."

Sebastian didn't remember most of his time at the hospital, but knowing she'd been there, so dedicated to making sure he was okay, made him feel better. He'd never had someone like that in his life before. And yet he'd managed to ruin it the moment he'd woken up. "Yes, well, once she determined I was okay, she left and said she wasn't coming back. I was just being optimistic that she'd changed her mind."

"What did you do?" Finn said in his usual accusing voice.

Sebastian shrugged it off. "I suppose I deserve that," he admitted. When things went wrong around the office, it was typically Sebastian's doing. He'd overload the breaker and cause a building-wide blackout. He'd set off the smoke alarm with his latest project and sent everyone marching out to the street while the fire department searched the building. Honestly, there were times where he wondered why Finn wanted to be his business partner. Or even his friend. But sometimes you had to overload the breaker to achieve greatness.

"She was sick with grief when I saw her at the hospital the first time. That woman loves you and cares about you very much. If she isn't here with you this very moment, you screwed up pretty badly."

"Okay, yeah, I screwed up," he said. "I didn't tell her about…well, anything. Including my heart condition. She said I was shutting her out. I guess I was."

"Why would you do that? She's by all accounts an amazing woman. I know her family, too. You don't drive a woman like that away when she loves you, Seb."

"I don't know why I did it. I guess it's just all I know how to do. I'm not a relationship guy. I'm an engineer. A pioneer in medical technology. I don't know how to be that and a man in a serious relationship. Is it even possible to be both at the same time?"

Finn chuckled and shook his head. "You'd better figure it out or you're going to be a lonely old man. I can't have you coming to my house for the holidays every year for the rest of your life. Eventually you're going to become our creepy uncle Sebastian."

"You're the one that invited me to your family Thanksgiving," Sebastian pointed out in a bitter tone.

"Of course I did. Otherwise you would've been at the office working. Or sitting at home eating who knows what with a plastic fork. If you're going to shake up your life, you've got to make a lot of changes."

Sebastian was used to his fair share of lectures from Finn—it was one of the side effects of working with a doctor—but for the first time in his life, he was actually listening to what his partner had to say. "Okay, fine. Fix me, Yoda. I'm a ball of clay in your hands. Turn me into a pastier, hairier but more charming version of you."

Finn ran his palm over his shaved head and twisted his lips in irritation. Fortunately he was used to Sebastian after years of working together. They were very different, but they complemented each other well. Sebastian's inventions wouldn't have been nearly as successful without Finn there to guide and market them. And Finn probably would've settled into some nice, boring dermatology practice on the Upper East Side if he hadn't had Sebastian pushing him to do more important things with his life.

"You've got to take better care of yourself, for one thing."

Sebastian couldn't help rolling his eyes. "Thank you, Dr. Obvious. But not all of us can be hunky Shemar Moore look-alikes with chiseled abs and muscular thighs like tree trunks."

"You think looking this good is easy?" Finn quipped. "It takes a lot of work. I'm at the gym five days a week. While you're getting junk food delivered to the office, I'm drinking protein smoothies or bringing in grilled chicken breast and kale salad for lunch. Life is a series of choices. You've just got to make better ones."

"You sound like my nutritionist," Sebastian grumbled. He'd already met with her and had his first cardiac rehab appointment. Basically he'd just walked on a treadmill while they'd done an EKG and monitored his blood pressure. It would get harder from there. As for the nutritionist, she'd decided to sign him up for a meal delivery service while he was recuperating. There was going to be a lot of lean protein and vegetables he couldn't recognize in his future.

Finn crossed his muscular arms over his chest. "I might know what I'm talking about, Sebastian. I *am* a doctor, you know."

"I know. And listen…" Sebastian leaned forward and rested his elbows on his knees. "For all my blustering, I am taking this all to heart. I know this is serious and I'm changing. I want to change. At this rate, I won't live long enough to be your kids' crazy uncle Sebastian, and I know that. I've always had this drive in me and succeeding was more important than anything else, including my own health. But you were right."

Finn held up his hands to halt the discussion. "Wait. Repeat that please. I want to cherish it."

Sebastian smirked at his partner. "You were right, Finn! Anyway, I'm trying to be serious for a moment here. My work is important, but I'm not helping anyone if I'm too sick to continue. I can't sacrifice my life, my health or my relationships to make my inventions a reality. There's more to life, and I realize that now. I realized it the instant I hit the ground."

He shook his head, thinking back to that night as

he'd stared down the barrel of Josie's gun and felt his chest tighten like a rubber band was wrapped around him. "It was the scariest moment of my life. As I went down, I looked at Harper and realized what was happening and how serious it could be. My life could've been ending. In those few seconds, all I could think of was that I'd never told Harper that I loved her. I was going to die and she was never going to know. I tried, but then I passed out."

Finn listened silently, a pained expression on his face. "That sounds horrible. Why didn't you tell her the first chance you got at the hospital? It might've changed everything for the two of you."

"I don't know. I've kicked myself over how that whole thing played out. I was so disoriented at first and before I could get my bearings, she was laying into me about keeping secrets. I instantly went on the defensive and then she was gone. But she was right, I wasn't telling her things. I have so much I need to share with her. But I need to start with how much I love her. That's the most important part."

"Wow," Finn said. "It's true. You've really fallen hard. I can see it in your face when you talk about her. I wasn't sure I'd ever see the day you looked up from your notebook and noticed someone other than a client. And to fall in love… If you can fix this, you might beat me to the altar. Maybe I can be your kids' crazy uncle Finn."

"Shut up," Sebastian groaned. "You've got women

lining up outside your apartment. If you could just pick one to keep, you'd be married in no time."

Finn laughed. "Probably so. If you're serious about wanting to marry Harper, maybe I'll catch the garter at your reception. You never know what can happen then."

Sebastian's expression instantly sobered. "I am serious about marrying her. I'm serious about all of this. I want to get my health in order so I can go to her and feel confident that I'm not selling her damaged goods. Then I want to tell her how I feel and, hopefully, she feels the same way. If she does, I'm going to propose right there on the spot. Time is too precious to waste. I don't want to give her the chance to slip away from me again."

"If you're really planning to propose, I know a good diamond guy. I could give him a call and have him bring some pieces here to the apartment."

That was a relief. Sebastian didn't even know where to start when it came to that. He couldn't name the four Cs if his life depended on it. "Set it up. I've still got to talk to her father and ask permission, but I want to move forward on everything. I want it all in place when the time comes."

"Sure thing." Finn picked up his phone and typed in a few things. "I'll have him text you."

"Perfect. It feels like everything is falling into place. I just have one more little thing to do first."

"What's that?" Finn asked.

"I have to figure out where Harper lives."

Twelve

"Come in."

Harper took a deep breath and turned the knob that led to her grandfather's study. She had been fearing—dreading—this moment since she was twenty-two years old. Now here she was, a woman of almost thirty years, and she felt as nervous as ever.

It was easy to be brave in Ireland when she'd been thousands of miles away from the consequences of her poor choices. With Josie having disappeared and the blackmail behind her, Harper knew she had to face her grandfather and the reality she'd avoided all this time. She had to tell him she was broke. Odds were that he'd probably already heard the news by now, but she'd wanted to tell him in person as soon as she had the chance.

"Afternoon, Grandpa."

The elderly man looked up from his desk and smiled at the sight of his only granddaughter.

"Harper! What a surprise! You're looking lovely, as always. For a moment I thought it was your mother standing there. You certainly have come to look so much like her as you've gotten older."

Harper gave him a hug, ignoring the tears in his eyes as they both thought about the woman who'd been taken from them too soon. As she sat, Harper realized that she was older now than her mother had been when she died. It was hard to believe. Life could be so unfair sometimes. It made Harper feel foolish for wasting all her emotional energy on such silly things when her mother had been facing her own death and leaving her children behind at the same age.

"To what do I owe this visit?" his asked. "I didn't expect to see you before your birthday. The big one is coming, isn't it?"

Harper smiled and nodded. "Yes, I'll be thirty."

"I suppose you'll have a big party to celebrate with your friends. Blow some of that inheritance on expensive champagne?"

She winced and shook her head. Considering everything that had happened over the last week, she hadn't planned anything. Turning thirty was depressing enough. Add that she was now going to be single and broke going into her thirties and she couldn't gather up much reason to celebrate. "Not exactly. That's why I came by to see you today. I needed to talk to you about my trust fund."

"Can't wait until the end of the week for the money?" he asked with curious gray eyes. "I suppose I could loan you a few dollars until then."

"No, Grandpa," she said, reaching out to stop him from pulling out his wallet. "I'm not here to borrow money. I'm actually here because I needed to tell you something."

His brows went up in surprise and he eased back into his leather chair. "Okay. What is it, Pumpkin?"

She took a deep breath, trying to figure out how she was going to tell him the truth. Pumpkin had screwed up. She'd thought that losing out on the money would be the hardest part, but she was wrong. Telling her grandfather what she'd done was far worse. The sun had risen and set on Harper as a child as far as he was concerned. He would be so disappointed.

"I'm broke, Grandpa."

He narrowed his gaze at her, visibly trying to piece together what she meant by that. "Broke, you say?"

"Yes. I've been keeping it a secret all these years because I was embarrassed and I didn't want to lose the rest of my trust fund. But I'm coming clean. I blew all the money when I was in college and I've been faking it ever since."

"So all these years…you never once asked for money. Your father didn't have any. How did you get by?"

Harper shrugged. "Like everyone else. I worked hard. I saved every dime I could instead of blowing it like I would've in the past."

"But no one knew the truth? Not even your brother?"

"No, I didn't tell anyone. Not Oliver, not Daddy. I didn't want anyone to know, especially you."

"If that's the case, why are you telling me this now, Pumpkin?"

Now it was her turn to frown. "Because I should be honest. You added the provision that said if I mismanaged the first payment, I wouldn't get the second. And I blew it. I wanted—no, needed—to tell you the truth, so you can have your financial manager do something else with the money. I've forfeited my share."

Her grandfather reached for the candy bowl on the edge of his desk. He grabbed a soft caramel and handed a second one to her. For as long as she could remember, he'd always had caramels in his study. He unwrapped the candy and chewed it thoughtfully. Harper could only hold on to hers. She was waiting for his response. The rebuke. The disappointment. For him to announce that he was donating her inheritance to a charity.

But he didn't. He just chewed his caramel and watched her. Finally he said, "Something else is wrong. What is it?"

"You mean aside from throwing away twenty-eight-million dollars?"

He nodded. "That's just money. Something else is bothering you. Something more important."

Sebastian. Could that be what he saw? "I've just had a rough week, Grandpa. Nothing has been going my way, be it my love life or anything else. Someone tried to blackmail me and they stole Mama's sapphire necklace when I didn't pay them in time. The guy I love lied to me and I don't know what to do. Really, losing the money is just the latest thing to come up. I'm not having a big birthday celebration. I don't feel much like celebrating."

"Tell me about this man. You said he lied to you."

She nodded. "He kept me in the dark about so many things in his life. I worry that he can't open up to me. Why would he keep things from me?"

"Why would you keep your friends and family in the dark about your own situation, Harper? I imagine you'll find the answers to your questions about your gentleman in your own motivations."

"I was embarrassed. I didn't want anyone to know I could be so stupid. They might treat me differently." As she said the words aloud, she realized her grandfather was probably right about Sebastian and his secrets. Would she have treated him differently if she'd known he was physically fragile? Perhaps. Was he embarrassed that he'd let his drive get in the way of his health? Probably.

Since they'd started out as a week-long fake romance, there'd been no reason for him to tell her those things. Honestly, if she hadn't been blackmailed, she wouldn't have confessed her own truths to Sebastian. Why would she expect him to do the same?

They had a lot to learn about each other. A week wasn't nearly enough time to peel back all the layers and expose the secrets shared with only the most intimate of partners. She'd overreacted out of fear, she knew that now. Seeing Sebastian lying on the ground surrounded by EMTs...the sirens, the wires, the shouting... It had been all so unexpected, so scary. Josie and the gun hadn't been important anymore. All that had mattered was Sebastian.

She'd almost lost him in the moment and she hadn't understood why. Then she'd turned her back on him and walked away—losing him for certain—just for doing the same thing she'd done her whole life.

She was a fool.

"Harper, why do you think I added that provision to your trust?"

She turned back to her grandfather and shook her head. "To scare me straight? I was a spoiled little diva. I'm sure you didn't want me to make the same mistakes as Daddy did."

"That's a little harsh," he said. "You just didn't know what it was like to go without. You didn't grow up poor, like I did, so you didn't have the appreciation for it. That wasn't your fault. But you have it now, don't you?"

Harper chuckled bitterly. "Most certainly. I kick myself every day for wasting what I had. I think about what I could've done differently. If I'd been smart or industrious like Oliver..."

"You don't have to be like your brother. He's one of a kind, and so are you. Let me ask a different question. If you were to have a second chance and someone handed you that two-million dollars over again, what would you do?"

She didn't even have an answer at first. "That's hard to say, Grandpa. I'd probably go wild and prepay my co-op fees and utilities for the next year. Stick the rest in the bank for a rainy day."

Her grandfather's old, weathered lips curled into a smile. "Okay then." He reached across his desk for his cell phone.

Harper was confused by his response. "Okay what?" she asked.

"Okay, it's time to call my estate manager and discuss releasing the rest of your trust fund."

"What do you mean, *release it*?"

He reached out and patted her hand. "Happy birthday, Harper. I'm satisfied that you've grown into the mature, responsible woman I've always known you could be. And as such, you're about to be twenty-eight-million dollars richer. Now go find this man you're in love with and plan a proper birthday celebration."

Sebastian walked into the lobby of Harper's building as though he were approaching the X on a treasure map. Finding where she lived hadn't been an easy task. To ask for it from her friends was to admit he'd never been to her home before—an incredibly suspicious fact considering they were dating. But without any other options, he'd had to confess the truth about their fake relationship to Emma when he'd hunted her down at FlynnSoft. But it was only when he'd told her that he was hopelessly in love with Harper, for real, that she'd given him the address for Harper's building.

He was in the process of signing in at the front desk when he heard a voice from over his shoulder.

"She's not home."

Sebastian paused and turned to find Harper standing behind him with a full bag of groceries in her arms.

"That's a shame," he said. "I really wanted to talk to her about something important."

Her blue-gray eyes searched his face for a moment. "Something important, huh? Well, maybe I'll let you up and you can wait for her. I'm sure she'll be interested in hearing what you have to say for yourself."

Ouch. Okay. "I'd really appreciate it."

Harper smiled and headed toward the elevator with him in her wake.

Sebastian hadn't been sure what kind of reception he would receive after the way they'd parted at the hospital. So far, it had been pretty neutral, but he was going up to her apartment. She could've just turned him away. That was something.

Running into his arms and kissing him would've been another option, but he may not deserve that. He had a lot of apologizing to do before hugs and kisses would be on the agenda. Her semi-frosty reception proved that much.

When they stepped into her apartment, Sebastian got his first real dose of what Harper's life was like. It was a nicer place than he had—a remnant of her old life—decorated with some familiar and inexpensive IKEA pieces. As she set her groceries in the kitchen, he noticed a nice bottle of champagne and a couple pouches of ramen noodles. He supposed she had learned balance over the years.

Sebastian hovered awkwardly at the entrance of the kitchen as she put away her groceries. He was waiting for the invitation to talk, but she hadn't given him one yet. He wanted to sit and look her in the eye, not try to apologize while she was distracted with chores.

Finally she folded the paper sack and looked at him. "Do you want a drink? I want a drink."

"I'm not really supposed to," he admitted. He really wanted one—it would ease the tension—but he was working on a new healthy lifestyle. Day drinking two weeks into the plan would doom him to failure. "Some water would be great, though."

She eyed him for a moment before she nodded and pulled two bottles of water out of the fridge. She handed him one and pointed to the wall. "Let's head into the living room. People always congregate in the kitchen and I hate that."

Sebastian backed out of her way and followed her lead into the open and airy living room. She had comfy couches, a few nice pieces of art he recognized and a decent-size, flat-screen television on a shelf. There was a wall of books on one side of the room and a wall of windows on the other. From where he was, he could spy a glimpse of green—Central Park—a few blocks away.

"Have a seat," she said as she settled onto the couch.

He opted for the oversize chair just to her right, facing her. Their knees almost touched as they sat, but he kept his joints to himself for the moment, no matter how badly he wanted to touch her. "Thanks for talking to me, Harper."

She shrugged and opened her water. "The last time I saw you, you were on death's door. I was hoping to hear you were doing better."

"I am," he said proudly. "I've been going to cardiac rehab three times a week and they've started me on a new lifestyle program that will make me more mindful of what I eat and how much rest I get. It's made a huge difference already."

Harper listened to him talk but nothing more than a casual interest lit her eyes. "I'm glad to hear that."

"Me, too. Going forward, I know I can't let my work overtake my life. I want more than a career and a string of patents under my belt. I want a life, too. A wife. Maybe a family."

That got her attention. She sat more upright in her seat, her brows knitting together in thought. "That's a big change for a workaholic bachelor. What's going to keep you from losing yourself in your work again and this time ignoring your new family instead of just your health?"

She didn't think he could change. "I'm not going to ignore you, Harper. I couldn't possibly."

"I didn't mean me," she said. "I just meant in general. Old habits die hard. Like keeping secrets. Trust me, I know."

"I'm sorry I lied to you. It wasn't that I didn't trust you with the different aspects of my past. I was just… embarrassed. You understand that, don't you?"

"Of course. But I told you everything, Sebastian. You told me almost nothing."

"If you hadn't been blackmailed by Josie, would you still have told me? Or was it only out of necessity?"

The self-righteous expression on her face softened a little. Her gaze dropped to the cap of her water bottle as she fidgeted with it. "And then I find myself clutching your unconscious body in the middle of a parking lot, screaming. When the ambulance arrives, I can't tell them your medical information. I can't say if you have a history of cardiac problems. I know literally nothing. You could've died and there was nothing I could do to help."

"I shouldn't have put you in that position. I never dreamed it would happen again or I would've said something."

Harper nodded. "I understand we started off with the whole fake relationship thing, but that's over. The wedding trip is over and now this is real life, Sebastian. Real feelings. We're not playing a game any longer. I need to know the truth."

"About what?"

"About *everything*. I want to know everything you've been keeping from me before I can consider continuing this relationship."

"Right now? You just want me to lay out my whole life story right now?" He had an engagement ring burning a hole in his pocket. He was desperate to hear her say yes and move forward, but Harper wasn't having it.

She sat back against the couch cushions, making herself visibly more comfortable. "Do you have somewhere you need to be, Sebastian? Work, perhaps? It's a Saturday, but who knows with you."

"No," he insisted. "There's nowhere I need to be but right here, right now. I'll tell you whatever you want to know if it will make you feel more comfortable in loving me. Because I love you, Harper. I've never let myself love a woman before. I'm not sure I'm going to do things right, but I can't help how I feel. I'll do anything you want me to if it means you'll tell me that you love me, as well."

Harper's jaw dropped at the first mention of the word "love" and stayed there until he was done speaking. "Well, why don't you start from the beginning? You've never said much about your family or where you grew up. Just about your brother's accident."

Sebastian nodded and sat back in his seat, ready to tell her whatever she wanted to know.

"I grew up poor," he said. "And so we're clear, not the kind of poor you've been. I mean dirt poor. Oldest-trailer-in-the-trailer-park poor. I never owned a new pair of shoes until I went to college and bought them myself. Until then, every bit of clothing I'd ever had was my brother's hand-me-down. My parents did everything they could to get ahead in life, but there was always something on the next horizon ready to knock them back down.

"When my brother and I were old enough, we worked to help make ends meet. Kenny worked at the burger place near our high school. I liked to tinker and helped my dad with fixing the car and such, so I ended up working at a shop that fixed old lawnmowers and small engines. If I could, I'd mow people's lawns after I fixed their mowers, too, for extra cash. Every penny went to my parents. For a while, we were doing okay. My dad got a promotion, my brother graduated from high school and started working full time. Then he had his accident."

Harper was watching him speak so intently, he wondered if she was even breathing. He shook his head and sighed. "We had insurance, but Kenny fell off the plan when he graduated. He didn't have any at work yet, either. There was a little coverage from the owner of the ATV, but it wasn't nearly enough. He spent my entire senior year in hospitals and rehabilitation centers. The bills were crippling. My mom had to quit her job to stay home and take care of him, making it worse."

"How awful," she whispered.

"I was determined to do more than just rebuild lawnmowers my whole life. I wanted to make something of myself so I could help my parents and my brother. That's what drove me. I worked as much as I could after his accident, and the only money I ever kept for myself was enough money to apply to MIT and take my entrance exams."

"How are they now?" Harper asked.

Sebastian finally found a reason to smile.

"They're great. With my first million, I bought my parents a real house in Portland that was near the doctors and specialists Kenny sees regularly. It's nice, but not too big for them to maintain, and it's fully wheelchair friendly so my brother can get around. I bought them an accessible van and I send them money every month to help take care of things. My dad continues to work out of pride, but he should be retiring in a few years."

Harper smiled and reached out to put a hand on his knee. "I'm glad to hear it."

"We've all come a long way. It took a lot of hard work to get there. I don't regret it or the toll it took on my health to get there. I just know I need to do better going forward."

"I can understand why you did what you did. To start with nothing and build a company like yours is amazing. I bet you look at someone like me, who squandered a fortune, and resent the hell out of it."

Sebastian shook his head. "I don't. Everyone comes from a different place, but that makes them who they are. You made your mistakes and you grew from them. You owned them. I'm not sure I'd be strong enough to stand up and do what you did at the wedding. Even with the money I've made, giving up almost thirty-million dollars is heartbreaking."

"Well, actually, it turns out that I didn't."

He frowned at her. "What do you mean?"

"I spoke with my grandfather. I came clean about the whole thing. He decided I'd learned my lesson and gave me the money anyway. That's why I bought the champagne. Today is my birthday. My grandpa wanted me to throw a big party but I wasn't ready for all that after what happened in Ireland. I thought I might have a little celebration by myself. Would you like to join me?"

Sebastian smiled. "I would." He wouldn't have more than a sip since he was trying to be good, but he would certainly toast to her birthday.

They got up and went to the kitchen where she poured two champagne flutes. Back in the living room, they sat, this time both of them on the couch together.

"Happy birthday, Harper," he said, raising his flute. "I'm glad I was able to be here today to celebrate with you. I wasn't sure if I would have the chance to tell you that. Or any of the other things I said to you today. Thank you for giving me the chance."

Harper smiled and clinked her glass against his. "Thank you. This isn't how I imagined my birthday, but it couldn't have been better, really. I've learned a lot about myself the past few weeks. Without Josie trying to blackmail me, I might not have realized that I could get by on my own. Or that I didn't need money and fancy cars to define me. I also wouldn't have realized how important you are to me, too."

Sebastian's heart stuttered in his chest and this time it had nothing to do with his clogged arteries. He set his untouched drink on the coffee table. "I'm sorry I didn't know it was your birthday today. I would've brought you a present." He reached into his pocket. "Instead, all I have is this."

Her gaze locked on the blue box and her jaw dropped once again. "What…" Her voice trailed off.

"I told you before that I love you, Harper. And that I'm ready to find some balance in my life. But what I left out was that I want to find that balance with you. Just you. Life is too short to hesitate, and I can't risk losing you again."

Sebastian slid off the couch onto one knee and opened the box to display the emerald-cut halo ring inside. "I promise that I won't keep secrets from you anymore. I promise I will never make my work seem more important than you or our family. You are the most important person in my life, Harper. I never knew I could love someone the way that I love you. Please do me the honor of being my wife, Harper Drake."

He looked at her in time to see her eyes flood with tears. "Yes," she whispered with a smile that spread from ear to ear.

Sebastian slipped the ring onto her finger and squeezed her hand in his. They stood and she leaped into his arms. He pulled her tight against him and kissed his fiancée for the very first time.

This was the start of their future together. A future he almost didn't have, but that he would cherish with Harper for as long as he could.

Epilogue

"**M**erry Christmas, everyone!"

Harper heard the commotion at the door and rushed out of the kitchen to see who had arrived. She was excited to host her first Christmas with her family and Sebastian's family all together.

Sebastian was hugging his mother as she came through the door. His father was right behind her with arms full of presents. And in the back was Kenny. *Standing.*

With the help of Sebastian's exoskeleton prototype, his brother moved in a slow but steady pace through the doorway with a wide grin on his face. He looked almost as happy as Sebastian himself.

Nothing could match his excitement. This was the culmination of his dream. The best Christmas gift he could ever give his family. She knew watching Kenny walk across the room and sit by the fireplace unaided was the greatest present Sebastian could ever receive.

It was his sketches from Ireland that made the difference. He didn't realize it at the time, but once he returned to his lab, Sebastian had a breakthrough. She could tell it pained him to come home at a reasonable hour each night when his mind wanted him to keep pushing, but his goal had still been achieved in the end.

The two families were introduced and everyone gathered with drinks and appetizers in the living room. Harper was just about to return to the kitchen for more eggnog when Sebastian caught her eye.

He reached under the tree for a gift and gestured for Harper to follow him down the hallway to their bedroom. "I wanted to give you this now," Sebastian said once they were alone.

"Now? It's only Christmas Eve."

"Please open it."

Harper sighed and accepted the beautifully wrapped present from her fiancé. He'd already given her such a beautiful engagement ring, she felt guilty accepting a present from him. She opened the golden foil lid and found a collection of sparkling items wrapped in tissue paper.

A sapphire necklace. A ruby tennis bracelet. Diamond earrings. An aquamarine cocktail ring. Emerald cufflinks. An old pocket watch.

It couldn't be.

Harper's eyes grew wide as she looked down at the gift and back up at Sebastian. "This is my mother's jewelry. And your things, too. Josie stole all of this. How on earth did you get it back?"

Sebastian grinned even wider than he had when his brother had successfully walked through the front door of their apartment. "Well, it turns out that our little blackmailer went after someone else to make some cash. Instead of paying, they went straight to the police. All these items were found in her apartment when she was arrested. The cops contacted me last week because the jewelry matched the description in the police report we filed."

She picked up the pocket watch and looked at it in wonder. Harper had thought she might never be able to replace this special piece for Sebastian. "They said they couldn't find Josie."

"Apparently that wasn't her real name. But after she tried to blackmail Quentin—"

"My ex, Quentin?" she interrupted in surprise.

"Yep. When he got the threatening letter, he remembered what happened to you and led the cops straight to her door. Turns out her name is Amanda Webber. I hope she looks good in orange."

Harper smiled and handed Sebastian his great-grandfather's watch. "Merry Christmas, my love."

"Merry Christmas, Harper."

* * * * *

If you liked The Boyfriend Arrangement, *then go back to the beginning with Emma's story in* Little Secrets: Secretly Pregnant*!*

Cautious Emma cut loose once—once—at a party, only to find herself pregnant by her masked lover. She meets him again in the last place she expects...at work! He's the rebellious CEO of the company she's auditing. Now, can she avoid mixing business with pleasure?

And don't miss the other books about this group of friends:

Rags to Riches Baby
One Unforgettable Weekend

Available now from Harlequin Desire!

***

If you're on Twitter, tell us what you think of Harlequin Desire! #harlequindesire

Get 4 FREE REWARDS!

We'll send you 2 FREE Books
<u>plus</u> 2 FREE Mystery Gifts.

Harlequin® Desire books feature heroes who have it all: wealth, status, incredible good looks... everything but the right woman.

FREE
Value Over
$20

YES! Please send me 2 FREE Harlequin® Desire novels and my 2 FREE gifts (gifts are worth about $10 retail). After receiving them, if I don't wish to receive any more books, I can return the shipping statement marked "cancel." If I don't cancel, I will receive 6 brand-new novels every month and be billed just $4.55 per book in the U.S. or $5.24 per book in Canada. That's a savings of at least 13% off the cover price! It's quite a bargain! Shipping and handling is just 50¢ per book in the U.S. and 75¢ per book in Canada*. I understand that accepting the 2 free books and gifts places me under no obligation to buy anything. I can always return a shipment and cancel at any time. The free books and gifts are mine to keep no matter what I decide.

225/326 HDN GMYU

Name (please print)

Address   Apt. #

City   State/Province   Zip/Postal Code

Mail to the **Reader Service:**
IN U.S.A.: P.O. Box 1341, Buffalo, NY 14240-8531
IN CANADA: P.O. Box 603, Fort Erie, Ontario L2A 5X3

Want to try two free books from another series? Call 1-800-873-8635 or visit www.ReaderService.com.

---

*Terms and prices subject to change without notice. Prices do not include applicable taxes. Sales tax applicable in N.Y. Canadian residents will be charged applicable taxes. Offer not valid in Quebec. This offer is limited to one order per household. Books received may not be as shown. Not valid for current subscribers to Harlequin Desire books. All orders subject to approval. Credit or debit balances in a customer's account(s) may be offset by any other outstanding balance owed by or to the customer. Please allow 4 to 6 weeks for delivery. Offer available while quantities last.

Your Privacy—The Reader Service is committed to protecting your privacy. Our Privacy Policy is available online at www.ReaderService.com or upon request from the Reader Service. We make a portion of our mailing list available to reputable third parties that offer products we believe may interest you. If you prefer that we not exchange your name with third parties, or if you wish to clarify or modify your communication preferences, please visit us at www.ReaderService.com/consumerschoice or write to us at Reader Service Preference Service, P.O. Box 9062, Buffalo, NY 14240-9062. Include your complete name and address.

HD18

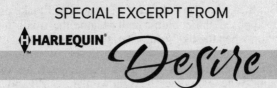
She was going to be interviewing Isaiah's potential wife.

The man she had been in love with since she was a teenage idiot, and was still in love with now that she was an idiot in her late twenties.

There were a whole host of reasons she'd never, ever let on about her feelings for him.

She loved her job. She loved Isaiah's family, who were the closest thing she had to a family of her own.

She was also living in the small town of Copper Ridge, Oregon, which was a bit strange for a girl from Seattle, but she did like it. It had a different pace. But that meant there was less opportunity for a social life. There were fewer people to interact with. By default she, and the other folks in town, ended up spending a lot of their free time with the people they worked with every day. There was nothing wrong with that. But it was just…

Mostly there wasn't enough of a break from Isaiah on any given day.

But then, she also didn't enforce one. Didn't take one. She supposed she couldn't really blame the small-town location when the likely culprit of the entire situation was her.

"Place whatever ad you need to," he said, his tone abrupt. "When you meet the right woman, you'll know."

"I'll know," she echoed lamely.

"Yes. Nobody knows me better than you do, Poppy. I have faith that you'll pick the right wife for me."

With those awful words still ringing in the room, Isaiah left her there, sitting at her desk, feeling numb.

The fact of the matter was, she probably could pick him a perfect wife. Someone who would facilitate his life, and give him space when he needed it. Someone who was beautiful and fabulous in bed.

Yes, she knew exactly what Isaiah Grayson would think made a woman the perfect wife for him.

The sad thing was, Poppy didn't possess very many of those qualities herself.

And what she so desperately wanted was for Isaiah's perfect wife to be her.

But dreams were for other women. They always had been. Which meant some other woman was going to end up with Poppy's dream.

While she played matchmaker to the whole affair.

Don't miss what happens when Isaiah decides it's Poppy *who should be his convenient wife in*
Want Me, Cowboy *by* USA TODAY *bestselling author Maisey Yates, part of her Copper Ridge series!*

Available November 2018 wherever Harlequin® Desire books and ebooks are sold.

Want to give in to temptation with
steamy tales of irresistible desire?

Check out **Harlequin® Presents®,
Harlequin® Desire** and
Harlequin® Kimani™ Romance books!

New books available every month!

CONNECT WITH US AT:

Facebook.com/groups/HarlequinConnection

 Facebook.com/HarlequinBooks

 Twitter.com/HarlequinBooks

 Instagram.com/HarlequinBooks

 Pinterest.com/HarlequinBooks

ReaderService.com

 HARLEQUIN®

**ROMANCE WHEN
YOU NEED IT**

PGENRE2018

Earn points on your purchase of new Harlequin books from participating retailers.

Turn your points into **FREE BOOKS**
of your choice!

Join for FREE today at
www.HarlequinMyRewards.com.

Harlequin My Rewards is a free program (no fees)
without any commitments or obligations.

MYR18